The (In)eligible Bachelors

The (In)eligible Bachelors

Ruchita Misra

RUPA
PUBLICATIONS INDIA

First Published 2011
Third Impression 2012

Published by
Rupa Publications India Pvt. Ltd.
7/16, Ansari Road, Daryaganj,
New Delhi 110 002

Sales Centres:

Allahabad Bengaluru Chennai
Hyderabad Jaipur Kathmandu
Kolkata Mumbai

Printed in India by
Nutech Photolithographers
B-240, Okhla Industrial Area, Phase-I,
New Delhi 110 020

For Sid who read about the Tiger,
For ma who saw the Sun,
For Diva who is a Genie,
And for chacha who owns a Crystal Ball

Contents

Thank you

Siddharth Vajpayee. Husband and best friend. For enduring the never ending jokes, for putting up with Bollywood inspired theatrics and for freaking out when I fall sick. Love. Sunshine. Cheer. You are my bright shining star.

RC Shukla and Kalaa Shukla. Dada and Nani. Dada, for transporting me to the magical world of monkeys with tails longer than the wall of China and three-inch-boys who outsmarted grown-up men. You are the best story-teller I know. Nani, because very simply, this was your dream.

Diva Kant Misra. Younger brother, staunchest supporter and 4 a.m. friend. For seeing this book through till the end. You are the nicest, kindest, funniest man I know. Stay that way. Love.

Anoop Mishra. Without your help in matters totally unrelated to the book, this book would have never seen the light of the day. Thank you. Extra thank yous for the jokes, the treats and the laughs.

Manjari Mishra. Chachi and friend. Thank you for taking out the time to go through the manuscript, cover and blurb. Your advice and encouragement is invaluable.

Kalika Vajpayee. Sister-in-law. For gifting me the laptop on which the entire story was typed and edited. Advance thank yous for the fly swatter promised next.

Latika Chawla. Soul sister. You reinstate my faith in the goodness of people. You are a rare species. Love.

Nivindya Sharma. Friend for over two decades and now London guide. For being there whenever I have been low and sad.

Nikhil Agarwal, Ritesh Agrawal and Khushboo Chovatia. The most amazing office buddies ever. Thank you for the gazillion laughs. Nikhil, your support for the book has been absolutely invaluable, thank you.

Rohan Dikshit, Rachit Kapoor, Neharika Neeraj Kalra, Vipul Janardan, JP Varnika, Archit Tewari and Parul Tewari. Thank you!

The team at Rupa. I cannot thank you enough for this wonderful opportunity! Thank you! Thank you!

My in-laws, Amita Bajpayee and Air Vice Marshal (Retd) Shyam Bihari Bajpayee, AVSM. Thank you for your love and support.

And finally, Rachana Misra and Nisha Kant Misra. Mom and Dad. Ma and Chacha. Love of my life and centre of my world. Cook and Chauffer. Often no and always yes. Love and Love. As a small token of the deep gratitude I feel for you two big throbbing hearts, I dedicate to you, Kasturi, the protagonist of my very first book.

And now, with the thank yous done, amidst the rolling of drums, I present to my readers, *The (In)eligible Bachelors*.

1

Home is, Unfortunately, Where Mother is

21 March 2009

'Beta, is there anything you want to tell me?' asked ma looking at me with a glint in her eyes I knew only too well. The knife in her hand was, befittingly enough, pointing right at me.

We were sitting at the dining table where mum was ferociously chopping vegetables for dinner. The innocuous looking dining table has become my personal torture cell over the last few days. It is where mum makes me sit to 'catch up' on the last two years I have been away from home studying at one of India's top B-schools.

'Yes. The lunch you cooked today was yucky,' I said nonchalantly flipping the glossy pages of a woman's magazine pausing only to admire the pout of a Bollywood actress whose name I could not quite recall.

'Kasturi!'

'Sorry, ma,' I said trying to sound apologetic yet feeling quite smug at my answer. I can be really smart with words you know.

'Kasturi, you know we are very understanding parents...we are fine if you have taken certain decisions on your own,' said ma very patiently.

'You can tell us everything,' added mum in a saintly voice.

'Yes, ma.'

'You know Bubbly aunty's daughter got married?' she inquired.

All that mom has been talking about since I came back has been Bubbly aunty's daughter's wedding. Bubbly aunty's daughter, Pinkie, cock-eyed and obese, but, as of today twenty-three and happily married.

'Yes ma.'

'...to her MBBS batch-mate,' she said with a special emphasis on the word 'batch-mate'.

'Yes ma, you have been repeating this stale piece news for an eternity now,' I groaned.

'Kasturi!'

'Sorry ma,' I cast down my eyes and yet again tried to look ashamed of myself as I giggled mentally.

'So is there anything you want to tell us?' said mom slowly as if speaking to some dimwit moron.

'Yes. The lunch you made yesterday was yucky too.'

I rolled off the chair breaking into laughter pretty much as soon as I finished talking.

30 March 2009

Rant Alert: I have not been home for a month yet and I am thinking of appearing for CAT again, only to go back to B-school. Mother, in her latest avatar, is impossible. She seems possessed with the lone, sinister wish of getting me married to the first guy she can lay her hands on.

I am intelligent, reasonably good looking, well educated and will soon be earning well enough. But of course, how does it matter at all? What is the use of it all if it does not serve the ultimate and supremely noble purpose of getting me a rich, handsome IIT/IIM husband who will forget his mother the second he sets eyes on me?

Since I have reached the ripe age of twenty-three (only for god's sake!) and have no boyfriend in tow, my mother, my mother's mother, my mother's sisters-in-law, my mother's sisters, my mother's brothers – all seem to think that I am doomed and run a high risk of ending up in an old-age home.

Even fat Pinkie managed to find a suitable boy who was also stupid enough to marry her.

OK.

I am not twenty-three.

I am now twenty-four.

Cue to break into inconsolable tears

3 April 2009

With a mother hell bent on getting me married come what may, hovering in the background, I have been forced to analyse the gravity of my situation.

Ever since I finished MBA and came back home with eighty-five kgs of books (no less, trust me), but no B-school batch-mate's hand in mine, mum has freaked out. It is interesting, however, that all the while I was in B-school, mum spent a considerable amount of time snooping around trying to figure out if I was doing the unthinkably low deed of seeing a guy. The perpetual 'Where-are-you? With-whom? Is-he-your-boyfriend?' routine if you know what I mean.

'Beta, where are you going?' she would ask each time I told her I was going out.

'Mum, for a movie.'

'With whom, beta?'

'Rahul, ma.'

'Is he your boyfriend?'

'No, ma.'

'You go out with him so often, he has to be your boyfriend,' mum would say.

'No, ma. He has a girlfriend off-campus.'

'...and still he goes out for movies with other girls!' Mom would say shocked at the wayward ways of Rahul.

'Ohho ma!'

'What ohho? You have to be extra careful with boys. They take undue advantage of girls. If he tries to hold your hand in the dark, just scream. Someone will come to help you,' mum would say breathlessly.

'MOM!'

'Promise me you will scream really loud or I won't give you permission to go.'

'Fine ma, I promise I will scream if Rahul tries to hold my hand,' I would say, just to bring her sails to tranquil shores. Permission for a movie? While I am in a B-school in a city about a thousand kilometres from where she is? Haah!

'*Pukka* promise beta?' mum would ask anxiously.

'*Pukka* promise, ma.'

'Bye beta. Call me when the movie ends and when you get in the auto. Talking of autos, beta, I read in the newspaper today that two girls were raped in an auto in Delhi…check the auto driver's face first – he should not look like a criminal then look at other stuff…'

The only escape then was to say 'hello' into the phone three to four times and then disconnect the call. Ask my mum and she will never recommend my phone connection to anyone. Calls get disconnected out of the blue, she would say to anyone who would listen.

Most importantly, inspite of all this, I now realise, that ma was quite hopeful (if not banking completely on the fact) of me getting some boy from B-school to meet the parents.

This has me very confused now. I must park this observation under 'Life is indeed stranger than fiction' category.

5 April 2009

'24, 157 cms, fair, beautiful, MBA, brahmin, non-manglik girl from a respectable family seeks tall, handsome, IIM/IIT groom'. I read out loud not quite believing my eyes. Dad had thrust this paper under my nose with a big smile on his face. Mum was standing right behind him with a smile wider than I would have imagined possible. She reminded me of the Cheshire Cat from *Alice in Wonderland.*

'Can you tell me who exactly is this 24, 157, fair, beautiful, MBA, brahmin, non-*manglik*, girl seeking an IIT/IIM guy?' I thundered.

'Of course it's you, beta! Do you want me to write "very beautiful" or is "beautiful" enough?' chirped ma exuberantly.

I felt blind with fury.

'What the hell are you guys trying to do with my life? You will NOT give this ad in the paper,' I screamed wildly, inexplicably hurt.

Mom bestowed a very patient smile upon me that I would have used only when dealing with an exceptionally dumb five-year-old.

'But we already have, beta. It will be in the papers next week,' ma said in a sugar coated voice.

'Maaaaa!' I wailed.

I glared at dad. He shrugged helplessly. His face looked tired because of the three surgeries I knew he had performed today. He did not need another showdown between mum and me at this hour. Poor fellow, he never could say much in front of ma anyways.

6 April 2009

Dad's mighty tickled with the concept of a matrimonial ad for his daughter. He has repeated this joke four times since yesterday. Twice to the guests when I was also present and twice just to me. It goes like this:

Man inserted an ad in the matrimonial section that read 'Wanted a wife'. He got a hundred replies in the next hour. All read 'Take mine'.

8 April 2009

10.00 a.m.

I am not speaking to ma nor do I plan to do that in the near future. War has, indeed been declared. She is in such a hurry to get me married that her way of dealing with things has stopped making any sense to me whatsoever.

I had a heart to heart with dad. He seems to understand but unfortunately like he has told me since I was knee high, he has absolutely no say in front of mum. Apparently, he tried all he could to postpone this calamity but March end was all he could manage. His new strategy is to be out of the house as often as is possible so that mum does not drag him into this war between me and her. Poor dad!

10.20 a.m.

I am not going to eat anything in protest of mum's behaviour. Hunger strike is my answer to her impossible ways.

10.22 a.m.

Mum is making kebabs. They smell delicious.

10.23 a.m.

But of course, I will obviously announce that I am not going to eat anything. Maybe that will make my mother take note of the fact that I am not exactly dying to marry straight out of B-school! Hunger strike! Who would have ever thought of that? It is a testimony to my strong will and resolve. I am the true daughter of the land of Gandhi.

10.30 a.m.

The smell of heavenly kebabs has filled the house and no matter where I go, I cannot help but smell them. How delicious and soft they must be and how they would melt in my mouth...ummm...

10.40 a.m.

I just set down my plate of yummy kebabs. Whatever else might be wrong with her, there certainly is no one who makes better kebabs than mum.

And, of course, needless to add, hunger strike will definitely begin tomorrow. No two ways about that one. After all I am the daughter of the land of the Mahatma.

9 April 2009

Dad has just announced that his hospital is organising a medical camp for villagers of a nearby village. It will last three days and he won't be home for that time. I heard him tell ma that he tried all he could to get out of it but the senior doctors would not let go of him. Mum has, very sweetly, promised to pack him lunch. How does dad get away with this? How?

Some three hundred people will get free treatment because of my matrimonial advertisement. At least something good is coming out of this war between ma and me. God bless dad. God bless his patients.

2

The Unsuitable Boys

12 April 2009

8.30 a.m.

The matrimonial ad should be in the papers today. I feel angry, hurt and humiliated. Also I don't care a penny for what happens now. I just don't care. Not even this teeny weeny, itsy bitsy bit. I hope no one will see my advertisement. I hope and pray no one calls up ma. That will be a good lesson for her.

9.00 a.m.

Not a single call so far. Great! Nothing could be better! Even mum is looking low. Very good. Very very good! Very very very good.

9.30 a.m.

None so far. Mum is pacing the drawing room like a crazed lioness. I love it.

10.30 a.m.

No call.

11.00 a.m.

OK, now I am just wondering why even a single person has not called? Apparently when Pinkie's mother had given Pinkie's matrimonial ad, some four people had called by 7.00 a.m.!

And Pinkie is cock-eyed for god's sake! Are normal eyed girls no longer in demand? Not that I want to get married or anything…

11.15 a.m.

Maybe mum should have written 'very beautiful'.

12.16 p.m.

This is turning out to be so embarrassing! Not a single call so far. Pinkie's mom who knew about the ad called up ma to ask her the count of calls so far. Mum lied that some twenty-five people have already called but none of them are any good so she would much rather not talk about them.

1.20 p.m.

The phone remains silent. Why does it not ring? What kind of a girl do the boys' parents want?

2.20 p.m.

Will I never get married?

3.00 p.m.

Will I die a spinster?

3.13 p.m.

Will my dead body rot for days in my apartment before neighbours complain of the stench?

3.18 p.m.

Will I be one of the old maids who say that her cat is her child?

3.30 p.m.

Someone help! Please!

3.35 p.m.

Dad is an absolute genius! He figured out the reason for not receiving a single call so far. Mum was sitting with the wrong mobile in her hand. The one that should have been used was lying somewhere without any battery charge. The phone was immediately hunted down, recharged and switched on.

Within seconds we started getting calls. All of us breathed a sigh of relief. I breathed the biggest sigh of relief.

Daddy is my superman. Yipeee.

8.00 p.m.

It has been an eventful day. Inspite of my anger at what ma has been up to, I must say I was indeed quite fascinated and very much interested in the calls that came in response to the ad. Well, I should be, after all it is my life they are trading over the phone.

14 April 2009

OK so, we now have a huge red diary in which mum is noting down the details of each boy whose parents have called in response to the ad. I feel an inexplicable sense of pride as I see page after page fill. Apparently a lot of people want their sons to marry a '24, 157, fair, beautiful, MBA, brahmin, non-*manglik* girl'. The quantity of calls is flattering. The quality is equally unflattering. By today morning mum was tired of taking the nonstop calls, so I offered a helping hand. After all I had been sneaking around enough calls to know exactly how the mother of the bride-to-be should speak. And I was confident I would do a better job than ma.

Also, I have now managed to devise a strategy to get rid of those guys you know you will not have any interest in. It is simple and I suggest be followed by anyone who is in a similar situation.

Sample conversation:

Me: Namaste namaste

Boy's father/mother: Ji behen ji, namaste!

both parties giggle meaninglessly for a couple of seconds

Me: Ji, bhai sahab.

Boy's father: Behen ji, you gave a matrimonial ad in Sunday's newspaper for your daughter. This call is in reference to that.

Me: Ji ji, thank you for responding. What does baba do?

Boy's father (after giggling himself, quite content at the excitement displayed by me so far): Baba did his class twelfth exams...and has done very well since...generally helping friends...after all everyone does a day-to-day job...one should try something different. He has a heart of gold. He is just so kind and religious. Any girl would be lucky to marry him.

No, I don't want to marry a guy with a golden or silver heart.

Me (sounding impressed): This is very nice, bhai sa'ab. How exactly does he help his friends? That's such a nice thing to hear.

Boy's father (sounding pleased): Ji, ji, he is a very hard-working boy, he invests my money in his friends' businesses. Some have worked, most have not. But he is learning, that boy, I know he will go a long way...

At this you dig out a red pencil and put a huge cross on the entry that has just been made for the now not so potential groom. *Time to put the strategy in place.*

Me: Very nice, very nice. By the way, bhai sa'ab, what is the *nari* of bhaiya?

(*Nari* is a concept you need to know nothing about. Except one thing. One crucial thing. As per Indian tradition, the bride and the groom should not have the same *nari*. Apparently it is quite a deal breaker. Grandmothers will much rather die than have their granddaughters marry a boy of the same *nari* even though they themselves are not really too sure about what exactly *nari* means or signifies.)

Boy's father gives the *nari* of his not-so-worthy son.

Me (grunting and sounding very disappointed and distressed, irrespective of what the *nari* is): Oh no! Bhai sa'ab, unfortunately my daughter shares the same *nari*!

Boy's father (alarmed, he was probably already debating whether it would be prudent to ask for the twenty lakh dowry right away or a Mercedes Benz would be enough): *Arre, Behen ji* ...let us not believe in all this. We are a very forward, contemporary family. We might even allow your daughter to work after the wedding. Why should we bother about things ancient?

Me (sounding forlorn): Bhai sa'ab, I had judged from your voice that you come from a forward thinking, modern family. Sadly we are not as modern. In fact, I personally don't believe in all this but my mother-in-law does. I cannot do anything that she does not approve of, you know how we must respect our in-laws.

Potential father-in-law: Yes, yes behen ji. That is very true, in-laws must be respected at all costs.

Me (in a sad, desolate voice): I wish we could have taken this further. Your family seems like a wonderful family.

Father-in-law (picturing a loss of near about twenty lakh rupees): I am also very very sorry!

Me: Ji, bhai sa'ab. Me too.

Bhai sa'ab: Me too

(Danger of nested looping of 'me-toos')

Me: Namaste bhai sa'ab.

Bhai sa'ab: Namaste behen ji.

Phew!

3

Shaadi.com Pics

15 April 2009

The world is rosy again. I need to somehow tolerate mother for just another month after which I will go to Delhi to start work at India Telcom Pvt. Ltd., India's largest Telecom company. Theirs was the most lucrative offer on campus and I was the lone candidate chosen. I cannot stop gloating about this. Anyway, coming back to mum, she is not being as big a pain as she has been in the recent past. She is content with how the groom hunt is coming along as a lot of people are calling up. I am content with how the groom hunt is coming along as none of them have sons who are any good, not even in my mother's rather lenient eyes.

So far so good.

29 April 2009

I think I spoke too soon. Mom has been incessantly discussing this guy from IIM–A for the past week. The first guy from any IIM mom has finally managed to 'catch'. Yeah, that's the word she used. I pity the poor guy who will end up being my mother's son-in-law.

I have also had the grand privilege of seeing the boy's photograph sent by his dad to my mom's email id, (Yes, mom has created an email id for the sole purpose of getting me married. She wanted to set the email id as *marrymydaughter@gmail.com*. I am not kidding. It took all my powers, latent and potent, to convince mother that this sounded horribly cheesy. She has finally settled for *brideofIndia@gmail.com*. Yes, that's the id. And no, I am not kidding.)

Anyways, the IIM-A 'catch' is dark, semi-bald and has a huge mole right below his nose. I could not take my eyes off his mole for some eight minutes. Again, no kidding.

Boy's father, two brothers and (wait for it) mother are all from IIT! I don't think I know anyone whose mother-in-law is an IIT-ian. I honestly don't. And so I already have an inferiority complex. Will they accept me even though I am not an IITian? Will they stoop to such lowness? Will they?

Haah!

5 May 2009

This has to be documented for the sake of posterity. I was made, rather forced to wear a sari and was dragged to a studio to get the shaadi.com photographs clicked.

I cannot believe I let mum get away with this one as well. She did the whole 'you-don't-love-me-enough' routine replete with tears, vacant eyes and the 'Mother India' look for the nth time and like an idiot, for the nth time, I fell for it.

Each time the basic routine remains the same.

1. She tells me what she wants me to do.
2. I refuse.
3. She repeats herself (tears brimming).
4. I refuse.
5. She looks pitifully at dad and asks him to ask me to do it.
6. I refuse.
7. Dad looks pleadingly at me and asks me to listen to ma.
8. I refuse.
9. Mum starts to wail and tears stream down her cheeks. She sits on the sofa hugging her knees with her head buried in her hands. And wails like there is no tomorrow.
10. I refuse.
11. She says, 'You don't love me enough, your father does not love me, your grandmother made life hell for me, your grandfather said so many acerbic things. I brought you into this world, I had to go through fifteen hours of labour, you don't love me enough.'
12. 'But mum...,' I say looking helplessly at the positively pathetic looking figure in front of my eyes.
13. 'I made tiffin for you each day of school, I ironed your shirt and tunic, washed your dirty socks that used to smell so bad, I carried you to school...you woke me up in the middle of the night till you were eight months old, both your buas used to fight with me each day, your grandmother made life hell for me, your father made life hell for me, you don't love me.'
14. 'Mum,' I say helplessly as dad plots and plans another outdoor camp for his patients.
15. She sniffs and cries and then cries a little more and then sniffs a little more. She looks quite forlorn. My heart melts. So I decide

to do what she wants me to. I go to her, pull up her face and tell her that I love her and will do what she wants me to do, but we cannot get the photographs clicked because the sari is not ready.

16. The tears are wiped hastily and the very next instant the familiar, triumphant smile is back. The sari is ready with the blouse and the accessories, she tells me looking so absolutely victorious that I am forced to cringe. Mum knows all too well that the 'you-don't-love-me-and-your-grandmother-made-life-hell-for-me' routine works without fail every bloody time.

So there I was, one hour later, standing with a poster of green mountains behind me and a pot bellied, frustrated looking photographer in front of me. As he fussed around and chatted with ma I concentrated on the big hair coming out of his ears.

Once the photographer was ready, I posed according to his instructions. By that I mean I looked up straight into the camera and tried to smile while managing a sari that suddenly seemed dangerously loose around my waist.

'Behen ji, baby is not giving the look,' complained the frustrated photographer to my mother pointing a thick finger at me. I grimaced. Couples back in B-school religiously referred to each other as 'baby'. Had to be my luck, to be called 'baby' by a fat, middle aged, bald photographer.

'Yes! You are right, she never gives the look,' Ma agreed as I stared indignantly at her, 'Give the look Kasturi!' Ma barked at me.

I was looking up and smiling. What else do these people want? In such moments I miss B-school the most.

'I am giving the look!' I said indignantly.

'No baby, you are not,' said the frustrated photographer. I cringed.

'Try looking more homely, more beautiful. Look like the daughter-in-law anyone would want,' suggested the ever frustrated photographer very unhelpfully.

'Do as bhai sa'ab is saying,' added ma equally unhelpfully.

'Bhai sa'ab is not telling me anything specific, ma!!' I wailed getting more frustrated by the second. How does one look like the daughter-in-law anyone would want? What the fish!

I parted my lips on one side, looked into infinity, opened my eyes wide and stared at the camera. I believe I looked insane.

'That's the look, bhabhi ji!' exclaimed the photographer, very excited as he clicked wildly lest I loose the look.

'See beta, when you listen to elders you do yourself good. That is why you should always listen to elders like me and photographer bhai sa'ab here,' Ma explained pointing towards the photographer who was by then swelling with pride.

Before we left the shop the photographer had offered to be the wedding photographer at 'baby's' wedding. Mum who seemed to be half in love with the fat photographer, blushed and laughed uselessly before saying, 'Yes, of course.'

Like I said, What the fish!

4

They, the People

10 May 2009

I am heading for Delhi. To start work and get away from mum! Yeayyyy!

12 May 2009

10:00 p.m.

Ma was getting teary-eyed today about me leaving home once again, this time for work. I too, felt a lump in my throat. Ma is not really *that* bad. I wish I could stay for two or three more weeks.

10.02 p.m.

On second thoughts, two-three weeks extra at home would be a bit too much, one would have been just fine.

14 May 2009

Wagon Ho! To Delhi! Wish me luck!

18 May 2009

Telecom India Pvt Limited, Delhi Office. That will go down in history as the first place where Kasturi Shukla ever worked! I am already in love with the huge, fifteen-storied building located in the centre of a city I have always loved. All management trainees will sit on different floors with their respective teams. I get to sit on the tenth floor and get a fantastic view of Delhi! The last three days have been very busy with the senior management giving us presentations on why Telecom India Pvt Ltd has been the best thing that ever happened to us. They expect us, MTs, to lead business and be part of all the exciting projects the senior management is involved in.

I love it! I will wear really fashionable formal clothes, sit in my cabin and be the hot chick who takes all the important decisions in office.

I cannot wait to start work!

20 May 2009

And with this, phase two of my life has begun! I have now been working for the last five days. It has been interesting, fun and tense all at the same time. I stayed in the office accommodation for the first two days where my roommate was this girl called Ananya who is an MT like me. In spite of the fact that our personalities are poles apart, we do get along quite well and had decided that we will house-hunt together. The very next day she found a house for us. Just like that. I think that is when I fell in love with her. She is low maintenance, looks grumpy all the time but is extremely easy going in every way.

21 May 2009

So while there are innumerable management trainees, I think I might be friends with two of them. The rest are either too vain or too irritating for my rather sophisticated tastes.

coy look

Here is the long list of people, I think I *might* like:

1. Ananya Goswami, HR, MDI

I have spoken about her earlier. She is not just a girl. She is a very boyish girl. Her mannerisms are so like that of a boy that she seems to be more of a boy than a girl. Tall at 5'8, the right words to describe her are 'strong' and 'lean'. She almost sounds like a handsome boy I can have a crush on. To boot, she has a razor sharp brain that works very well around all things related to computers and finance. An elite digerati, her nonchalance as she blew the arrogant IT head's head (hah!) with her questions during our session with him was just super wow. I had felt an indescribable urge to start clapping when she had finished with the IT head. One day she will, undoubtedly, be the pride of HR junta worldwide!

Extremely no nonsense, even to the point of being intimidating, she always speaks her mind. She has already called me 'too girly' with all my pink office shirts and sensible fake diamond studs. While of course I shall defend unto death anything pink, I cannot help but admire the fact that she does speak her mind.

I think I will like her.

2. Varun Agarwal, Finance from IIM-I

Interestingly, he is more of a girl than a guy! Thin and tall with sharp features, he jumps with a start each time Mr Pandey our assistant manager sneezes too loudly. We girls or at least the girly ones, giggle dutifully whenever Varun does that. Ananya just cringes.

Varun seems to be a typical finance guy and can happily drool over excel sheets the whole day. Nerdy and quiet but thankfully a big gossip monger, each canteen break with him has been a fascinating gossip session any girl in her right mind would die for!

Why do I like him? Well...because in spite of the gossip (which though is almost always juicy, is never mean) he seems to be honest and sincere and I like such people.

And with that the long list of people in office whom I even think I might like, comes to an end.

Anyways, the induction is now over and I have definitely had enough of why being in this company is the best decision I have ever taken in my life. I am, however, yet to meet my boss Rajeev Mehrotra. He has been on leave for this entire week but is expected to be in office sometime soon. For inexplicable reasons the word 'boss' brings to my mind the rather disturbing image of the frustrated photographer who took my shaadi.com pics. I am, and understandably so, quite nervous about meeting Rajeev sir. As they say, you don't work for a company; you work for your boss.

Ahem.

22 May 2009

Enter LSD aka Lakhan Singh Deodhar, the chief executive officer of Telecom India Pvt Ltd.

CEO of India's largest Telecom company.

Stout and pot bellied, the first thing about him that caught my attention were his missing teeth. All of us management trainees had lunch with him after his speech which was nothing short of spectacular. The speech mainly consisted of the following:

- Why the telecommunications industry is so great
- Why Telecom India Private Limited is so great
- Why is *he* is so great

In his presentation there was one particular section that intrigued me no end. It was called 'Quotes from Great Men' and was made up of three slides. The first one had a quote from Martin Luther King (he spent two minutes on it), the second one had a quote from Mahatma Gandhi (he spent one minute on it) and the third had his quote. Yes, *his* quote. The slide had his picture in the background and he spent some fifteen minutes talking about *his* quote. It was 'Love is god and god is love'.

That was no way his, I thought indignantly! I spent better part of first standard writing essays on stupid things like 'my home,' 'my pet' and 'my garden' and in each and every one of these I have used this line. Without fail, in each one.

Sample essay from Class One.

My Mother

I have one mother. Her name is Prabha Shukla. She is round and fat. Daddy called her a tent once. She did not cook for us for three days after that. She believes that love is god and god is love.

My mother shut me in the bathroom for two hours the day I brought the corrected copy back home and she had a chance to go through the essay.

Sample lines from sample essay on 'My Pet' also submitted in Class One:

My Pet

I have a pet dog called Moti who is a girl. People think I
call her Moti because she has white fur that looks like pearl.
But I call her Moti because she is fat. Moti believes that love
is god and god is love.

I think I was shut in the bathroom the day I got the corrected copy of this essay as well for some reasons totally unrelated to Moti.

Anyways coming back to LSD, I mean like come on, dude! Really, come on. That's a quote from you?

I was sitting with Varun and Ananya during the speech. I saw Varun stuff a handkerchief in his mouth. He tried to stop his laughter as LSD rattled on and on about why love is god and god is love. LSD discussed the human spirit, atoms and a variety of similarly weird things while the group of hungry management trainees disguised yawns and giggles into coughs and grunts. Ananya just glared at LSD.

Another important thing that happened was that all MTs, excluding me, were introduced to their managers excluding me. My manager, Rajeev, is still on leave. Not that I have any problem with this but I do think I am missing out on one great pleasure...bitching about my boss. All others are already knee deep into it. All I do is listen and hope that one day soon enough I will also be a part of this great bonding exercise.

23 May 2009

'And so my folks want me to meet all these guys while I am in Delhi and see if I like any,' I concluded with an adequately dramatic sigh. I felt quite like a girl ready to give up the happiness of her life for the sake of her parents. Pretty much like the heroine of a Bollywood movie from the seventies who lives in a hut and will do anything that the school teacher babu ji says.

Anu, Varun and I were sitting in the office cafeteria having lunch which had already taken up two glorious hours. In our defense, we all felt the need for a break, a relief from the excessive PPT making sessions and photocopying effort we had put in through the morning hours. Yes, that is what they were making us do after grand promises of making us lead business. I have not worked for a month and the bubble has burst.

I will someday write in detail about the myth that the so called training period for management trainees is. Someday. The only thing MTs end up getting trained in is how to not be trained in anything.

'Why?' asked Ananya breaking my line of thought.

'So that I can marry one of them!' I said.

'Why?' asked Ananya, her face expressionless.

'Because...errr...umm...because...one should get married,' I stammered.

'No, not at all,' said Ananya firmly.

'Umm...I am being forced to...,' I said.

'Do you want to marry?' she interrogated. I looked at Varun for help.

'No...not really,' I said feeling unsure.

'Then tell that to your parents,' she said.

'Well....ummm....'

Ananya gave me a dirty look that silenced my pathetic 'umm'-ing.

'So, Ananya, you tell us. What's your status?' asked Varun thankfully changing the topic.

'Status of what?' she asked.

'Your love life,' said Varun, reminding me of Pankhudi aunty. Pankhudi aunty had been mum's best friend till they fell out over a cup of turmeric powder or something. I firmly believe that in my engineering days Pankhudi aunty always knew I was going out with a boy even before I got to know that myself.

'Duh!' said Ananya.

'And that means...,' persisted Varun doggedly.

'I don't have one! And I do not have time for any stupid guy!' she said, dispensing an angry glance at Varun.

I had no doubt she meant it.

25 May 2009

Ananya is planning to rejoin karate classes.

Rejoin.

Karate.

I fear for the boys on this planet.

26 May 2009

Mum has been sounding very fishy of late. Dad is going for too many camps for my comfort. There is something wrong at home. I have no doubt about it.

I 'beautified' three presentations today. Till my boss reclaims his seat, this is what I spend most of my time on. B.Tech, MBA and now beautifying presentations. Well, such is life.

27 May 2009

All that I am doing in office is wasting time. Everyone around me is either working or staring at me because I am not working.

So much for leading the company and hence the country into change.

Sigh

5

Will I Marry Pita ji?

29 May 2009

Ma called today, very excited, as I was studying an exceptionally complicated powerpoint presentation that traced the journey of the Telecom sector in India. I just cannot stand another presentation that has the liberalisation of the Indian economy as its first slide. Frustrated with the liberalisation of India, I picked up the phone.

'Beta!' said a familiar voice the chirpiness of which immediately put me on high alert.

'Ma?' I asked suspiciously, 'What's up?'

'I have found a very nice boy for you! I will get you married to him!' came the excited response.

'What!' I said shocked, suddenly unable to breathe.

'I mean...go meet him...see if you like him,' she said patiently. I breathed easier. So unlike Kajol in *DDLJ*, my marriage has not been fixed by babu ji. I still had a chance at life. Wow!

'...Although I see no reason why you will not like him!' added my mother in a tone that made it very clear that if I came back without having fixed my wedding date and the template of the wedding card, all would not be good for me.

'I am busy,' I tried another tactic.

'No, you are not,' said my mum as if stating a well-known fact. I sighed deep and heavy as I realised how true her statement was.

'How do you know that?' I questioned nevertheless.

'If you are, you will cancel your prior engagement and go meet him,' she said with finality in her voice that disturbed me to the core. This was the same stern tone she had used throughout my childhood while ordering me inside the bathroom. I gulped at the not so pleasant memories from years ago that had just opened a flood gate of rather painful emotions mainly centered around hours in the dark, dank bathroom.

'Tell me about the boy,' I said, hoping to find something that would help me veto this devious plan my Ms Havisham incarnate mother had concocted.

'Very nice boy! Name is Amay! Twenty-eight, ISB pass-out, currently works with Citi Bank, rich IAS parents, no *nari* issue, no *mangalik dosh*,' she rattled off.

Yeah, right, no *nari dosh* and no *manglik dosh* make the boy perfect husband material. Of course, what else do you look for in a husband?

'Fine, I will see when I am free. Will meet up some day,' I said airily quite loathing the idea.

'No.'

'What no?'

'Not any day, tomorrow, you go meet him tomorrow,' she said.

What the FISH!!!

'Wear a salwar-kurta and if it is possible, please try "acting" shy,' came ma's salvo of instructions. In the ambush strategy typical of her, ma yet again took me unawares with every detail already planned.

She has also called up a beauty salon and fixed an appointment for a fairness facial treatment. With new found internet savviness, she has emailed the address and phone number of the salon to me! After my fairness treatment, I am *supposed* to check out FabIndia's latest salwar-kurta collection, buy one that I like (which should not have a 'very' deep cut neck, though slightly deep is permissible) and use it for all such 'trial meetings' with boys.

I shuddered. How many such 'trial meetings' had mum planned?

The conversation with mum soon became a one-sided affair. I stopped protesting quite early into the conversation and soon reduced my contribution to barely audible, *'haans'*.

By the time the call got over, I was extremely exhausted and resigned to fate.

30 May 2009

12:00 noon

I spent two long hours wailing to dad on the phone last night. He sounded so helpless and I wish he would take a stand in front of ma both for his good and mine.

Sigh

So, well, I did go to that beauty salon and did get the fairness facial which cost me ₹3500 of my hard earned money. ₹3500 for which I had spent hours slogging with powerpoint and the photo copier at work down the drain.

Unfortunately, I could see no changes in my face post the three hour facial but the beauty salon lady has promised a glowing radiant skin in effect after three hours. Give me three hours and I shall be the fairest I have ever been. That boy, Amay, he will be on his knees begging me to marry him by the time the evening ends, I am quite sure.

While waiting for my face to start glowing like it has never glowed before, I surfed the internet and carried out a basic level investigation on Amay. I checked him on Facebook and Orkut. Interestingly, he was nicknamed Pita ji at ISB. I saw some photographs of him and could well understand the secret behind him being nicknamed 'Pita ji'. He totally looked like one.

I am meeting Pita ji at 7 p.m. at Big Chill today. If nothing else, at least the food will be great!

Will I or won't I marry Pita ji? That is the question.

3.15 p.m.

OH-MY-GOD!

I am *not* a million times fairer and do *not* have *any* glow whatsoever. Instead, I now have three big, huge disgusting looking zits on my otherwise clear face. Two of them are on my cheeks and the third one sits bang in the middle of the bridge of my nose!

What if I really like Pita ji but Pita ji does not like me? What if Pita ji thinks that I am perpetually zitty and if he marries me we will have kids who will have zits all over their faces even when they are in their mid twenties? Oh noooooooo!

I made another emergency call to dad pulling him out of the Operating Theatre to fill him on the situation at hand. He says I am being unreasonably panicky (and I beg to disagree, three zits out of the blue on your face, the biggest one on the tip of your nose when meeting the first boy ever for potential marriage?).

Dad seemed to be quite confident that Pita ji will like me. Yeah, he actually said that, 'Beta, don't worry, I am sure Pita ji will love you!'

It kind of cracked me up. Dad calling a twenty something Pita ji.

31 May 2009

I had no energy left to write last night, absolutely no energy! Wait till I tell you all that happened.

So as I hurriedly made my way to the restaurant, late by almost twenty minutes, it took me little time to find Pita ji, thanks to the Orkut photographs for public view.

He was wearing a frown and spectacles. I, on the other hand, was wearing blue jeans and a sleeveless white cotton top. I had pulled my hair in a ponytail and used white clips. Ananya had lent me some concealer which she was anyways going to throw away. (Anu never buys cosmetics and if some unsuspecting person makes the mistake of gifting her some, she politely throws it away.)

I had used the concealer to disguise the three zits and felt quite confident that I had done a good job of it. Pita ji was wearing a blue and black check shirt, was tall though his shoulders were slim, had large goofy looking eyes and a mouth that looked like one that would break into a smile anytime. However, for the time being, he had a slightly irritated look on his face maybe because I had most impolitely kept him waiting for about twenty minutes. I could not decide whether I liked him or no.

'Hi, Amay?' I asked walking up to him.

'Kasturi?'

'Yes,' I said and took his extended hand. It was big and warm but the grip was too firm.

'Please have a seat,' he said.

We sat down and there was a moment of awkward silence. Neither knew what to say.

'So!' I said enthusiastically trying to start the conversation.

'So...,' said Pita ji raising his eyebrows.

'So?' was my intellectual contribution to the conversation.

'So...,' said Amay slowly.

I could envisage the nested loop problem. I think it was right then that I decided that Amay would not be the guy who would put the proverbial *'sindoor'* in my proverbial *'maang'*.

'Well...so how have you been?' I asked politely, deftly leading us out of the nested loop issue as he stared at me in the most blatant manner possible. I waited politely as he continued to stare. He seemed incapable of taking his eyes off my face! Does he, like all the other men on the planet, find me excruciatingly beautiful? Oh well, I do have that effect on guys, I thought to myself looking coyly at my nails. Always the same effect, I thought letting out a huge sigh and thinking about the rest of the female population. With me around, what chance did the poor things have?

'Is that a zit?' Pita ji asked in a low albeit incredulous voice as he continued to stare at my face. He pointed towards my nose as my eyes grew to the size of saucer pans. This could not be happening.

'What, where?' I pretended to not understand.

'That...that thing on your nose. That huge black thing,' he said as my head buzzed with gazillion sounds of protest. No, this could not be happening!

'It is not huge, it is not black and it is not a thing!' I said, getting very angry. How can a man ask a girl about her zits? A girl whom he has just met! A girl who might have ended up as his wife had he not asked this question!

'Okay it is not like ten feet in diameter but it's huge if you consider the location, it is taking up some twenty percent of the bridge of your nose,' was the unbelievable albeit perfectly logical and correct answer.

He stopped for two seconds and looked more intently at my face. He then pointed to my cheeks and added, 'Oh I can see another one…and another one…why do you have so many of them?'

I was horrified! My mum thinks I should marry this guy? No seriously!

'I think I need to go,' I said curtly, quite unwilling to discuss my zits any more. I was not going to take any further nonsense from this man who could not say one sentence without offending me. I am, after all, a woman of substance.

'Why? You've just come. You have not even eaten anything,' he said looking genuinely confused.

'I did not come here to eat. I came here to make a decision and that I have made. Good bye!' I said angrily.

I stood up. Amay stood up too. I think I had been a little loud as I could see some people staring at us.

'Bye. I will see you later,' I said firmly, 'or maybe not,' I very smartly added under my breath. I quite felt like a woman of the twenty-first century, standing up, literally, for what I believed in.

Imagining a camera zoom in to focus on me, with one glorious, swift, elegant movement, I swirled around and crashed full body into a waitress carrying two pitchers of Coke and two glasses of Big Chill's very famous Oreo milkshake.

The very next second we, and by 'we' I mean the waitress, myself, the two pitchers of coke and the two glasses of Oreo milkshake, were a miserable, sad, pathetic, centre-of-all-attention pile on the floor.

The Oreo milkshake, a personal favourite might I add, had drenched my shirt and hair. Chunky bits of oreos were stuck on my face and shirt. Coke spilt on my jeans had formed a puddle in the middle of the restaurant. Hair disarrayed, I lay semi-sprawled on the floor stunned into inaction. For a couple of seconds the earth stood still. No one moved an inch and everyone stared at us.

Then finally after what seemed like an eternity someone offered me his hand. That someone was not Pita ji, I checked immediately. I don't remember the face and in all probability did not even look up to see him. The only thing I remember about that hand was that it was large and warm. It also had a scar running right across it.

The hand with the scar pulled me up and a gruff but concerned voice asked me if I was OK. In the background the waitress who had gotten up without any help apologised profusely although this was certainly not her fault.

A lot of people had gathered around me and I spotted Amay amidst the crowd, resembling a fish, gaping with his mouth open. A particularly stupid looking fish.

As all of this started registering and as soon as I got on my feet again, which was a few seconds later, I lunged for my bag, yanked it from my chair, sprinted towards the door and dashed out of the restaurant. I could not have spent another moment there.

I had not in my worst nightmare thought that my first attempt at finding a husband would go so horribly wrong. I have never felt so humiliated except when I was caught cheating in class seven by our history teacher. Never ever since then. Never. Never. Never.

6

Mehrotra, The name is Mrs Mehrotra

6 June 2009

I am still trying to get over the whole Pita ji fiasco. I had to pull dad out of an emergency operation yet again to wail my heart out to him.

8 June 2009

Mum called today and I have just one question. Are all mothers like mine? If not, can I please please please exchange mine for another one? Any shape, size or colour will do!

She has apparently been speaking to Pita ji's parents who, by now, have a minute by minute account of all that happened at Bill Chill including my zits and the fall.

Soothing my nerves, still frayed from the incident, mum was happy to inform me that no one has been taking the issue seriously; apparently everyone had a great laugh with Pita ji's mum laughing most uncontrollably for ten minutes. Not to be outdone, my mother told me proudly that she ensured she was the one with the loudest laugh.

I cringed.

Mom then told me that she was intelligent enough to convince Amay's mom about the zits being a rare feature and that I have always had an exceptionally smooth skin. She brought to everyone's kind notice that my skin is very smooth and so is hers, thereby indicating that I come from a gene pool where glowing, zit-less skin is a given.

And like always mum kept the worst for the last.

'So when do you want to meet Amay again?' she asked casually, almost after I had bid her a relieved good bye.

'Meet what again?' I asked incredulously.

'Not "what", beta, "who"..."who",' she corrected me patiently.

'I am not meeting him again!' I said aghast. Visions of our last encounter still had me up in the middle of the night gasping for air.

'Of course you are! You were with him for nineteen minutes only and that is not enough to take such a big decision!' she added.

'How do you know that I was with him for nineteen minutes,' I asked belligerently. She was making it up. I too had no idea about the time I had spent with Pita ji except that it was an incredibly short meeting.

'Amay times everything! His mother told me about it,' she said primly.

Pita ji times meetings with girls and then tells his mother about it? What, no, I mean like really, what kind of an idiot is he?

'No, ma. I am not going!' I said flatly.

'No, beta. You are certainly going,' Mum said copying my tone. I just cannot stand her when she imitates my voice and tone.

'Ma…' I said

'Kasturi, this is not done. I have promised his mother,' Ma said, 'they are very nice people you know…Amay's dad and mum are rich IAS officers and they have five houses in Mumbai and Amay is their single child. It will all come to you…' she dangled the carrot in front of me. I mean like seriously. What does my mum think of me?

'Ok ma, I will go…' I said just to put an end to mum's incessant nagging…Also, like a bolt of lightning I had just had an idea that was nothing short of brilliant.

I will go meet him. But not alone.

Haah!

21 May 2009

7.00 a.m.

I have a meeting scheduled with my boss, Rajeev Mehrotra for 9.00 a.m. today. He is back from his break and is keen to meet me right away. And with this my honeymoon period at work comes to a sad end.

I am quite nervous about meeting Rajeev sir.

7.30 a.m.

Why could not his trip last for another glorious week? I think I was enjoying his vacation more than he had been. Why god, why? Why me all the time?

8.00 a.m.

What if I cannot stand him for one second?

8.30 a.m.

What if he is a big pervert?

8.40 a.m.

What if he has yellow teeth like LSD? Lakhan Singh Deodhar and his teeth are single handedly responsible for taking away all the shine I had associated with the epithet of 'chief executive officer'. The word is now yellow and smells bad.

8.45 a.m.

What if he overloads me with a lot of work?

8.47 a.m.

What if I have to shorten my 2.5 hour lunch breaks with Varun and Anu due to workload? The management trainee in me shuddered at the thought.

8.55 a.m.

What if he is a pervert with yellow teeth who gives me tons of work?

10.30 a.m.

So, with a multitude of rather unpleasant thoughts running inside my head, I walked into the meeting room at nine sharp. Rajeev was standing next to his table and was looking out of the window with his back to me.

'Morning sir,' I said confidently. I was ready to face whatever (good/bad/ugly/smelly) came my way.

Rajeev sir turned to face me in a slow Bollywood fashion. And in that one moment, I reeled and almost stumbled on nothing.

Because, I had just come face to face with the most excruciatingly handsome face I had ever set my eyes on.

Rajeev sir is over six feet tall with a broad muscular frame. His lovely brown eyes that seemed to be of a lighter shade than they actually are as the sun shone in the room, reminded me of a golden retriever I had when I was young. When he smiled, as he did to welcome me, his left dimple proudly presented itself to me. Chiseled features, eyes that bespoke of confidence and in a voice that seemed to belong to a Greek God, 'Hello Kasturi,' he said slowly, looking intently at me.

I felt blood drain out of my heart. 'Kasturi' had never sounded so exotically beautiful before.

'Hel...hello...sir...sir...nice to...to...meet you,' I stammered shaken by the glorious beauty of my boss. For some reason I could not believe it. Someone should have warned me, for god's sake! You cannot have a Lakhan Singh Deodhar and a Rajeev Mehrotra in the same office! What good is Varun with all his gossip if he did not know *this*?

'I am sorry, Kasturi, I was on leave. Did you face any problem? Have you been issued the company laptop?' he asked politely, coming closer.

I vigorously nodded my head not trusting myself to speak.

The conversation then drifted towards things official. He politely told me what he expected of me and what all I should keep in mind while working in this office.

I slowly regained my breath and composure and was, in some time, able to contribute constructively to the conversation with extremely intelligent 'yes's, 'ooh's, 'aah-I see's and 'of course's.

The conversation ended with a handshake that left me weak in the knees. I had to swallow hard a couple of times before

I felt convinced that all was good with the upper thoracic. As I walked out of the office, weirdly enough and in my humble defense I am not one of those empty headed girls, there was just one thing in my head.

Kasturi Rajeev Mehrotra

Mrs Mehrotra.

Mrs Kasturi Rajeev Mehrotra.

Sigh

That sounds perfect.

23 May 2009

I set loose my resident detective, Varun, to get me more information on my object of fascination. I got a text from Varun late after work when I was watching an episode of *Friends* on my laptop asking me to check gmail. In the inbox there was a mail from Varun with a PPT attachment. I opened the attachment and the first slide read as follows:

'Rajeev Mehrotra – a basic level investigative study'. It had a picture of Rajeev Mehrotra in the backdrop which I guess must be his Facebook profile picture.

I chuckled to myself as I pressed the next arrow. The slides contained a lot of basic information about Rajeev sir.

He primarily belongs to Delhi though he has lived in different parts of the world when he was younger. He has an engineering degree from France and has done his MBA from India. He speaks fluent French and Gujarati. He comes from a very well-to-do family and has no siblings. He joined India Telecom Limited three years back and has been awarded the Employee of the Year award twice since then. He is known to be quite popular in office.

There was a separate section called 'Things to investigate further'. There were two bullet points. One spoke about a tiny (font size 18) tattoo on the inside of his wrist. Apparently it says 'Teena'.

Hmm…

The second point had this to say:

> *Why is Kasturi Shukla, B. Tech and MBA from such reputed institutes, interested in a man who has done his MBA from – IPPM!*

7 June 2009

I was with Rajeev sir helping him with excel sheets this morning. I spent most of my time twisting and turning my head in weird directions to have a look at the tattoo. I had to 'accidently' drop a number of things to get an excuse to twist and bend all around. Finally I got to see, it. Teena, it said unmistakably. My heart sank.

'My mum,' he said smiling sheepishly when he saw my eyes drawn towards it.

What?

Mum?

Mum!

Mum as in mummy?!

That's the sweetest thing ever! Who gets his mum's name tattooed on his arm? Like my dad says, it is only a guy who respects and loves his mother who can love and respect his wife. I breathed easy.

8 June 2009

I am spending most of my office hours working on PPTs primarily because of Rajeev sir's surprisingly limited knowledge of powerpoint. He comes to my desk about five to six times a day to discuss matters related to powerpoint. I live my hours in office waiting for him to come by.

I caught him looking at me twice today. Admiring my beautiful face and exquisite features, maybe?

9 June 2009

How is it possible to be so handsome? How can someone, no anyone, walk so gracefully, talk so gracefully...even throw orange peels in the dustbin so very gracefully?

10 June 2009

The marketing team had an important meeting today with the CEO, Lakhan Singh Deodhar. We have such impromptu meetings some ten times a day but this one had been planned weeks in advance. Rajeev sir was supposed to present the marketing team's strategy for the next year. Since I make all his PPTs these days (in fact, unfortunately, for all the grand things promised during my induction, PPTs is all that I make in office!), I knew very well that he had no PPT to present. Unless of course, he had done all the work himself which I knew was a remote possibility. Intrigued, I waited for him to react as the clock ticked away dangerously.

About one hour later, he sauntered to my desk.

'Hey Kasturi!' he said with a broad, relaxed smile. He was wearing a half sleeved baby pink linen shirt and grey trousers. The diamond in his left ear glittered as the sun shone in from the window.

'Sir,' I said looking up and quickly closing the Facebook window.

'Hunt for last year's marketing strategy PPT. Change 2008 to 2009 everywhere, update the new markets entrants slide, change the background completely, shake up the order of slides and mail it to me. Cool?' he said raising one perfect eyebrow ever so lightly.

'Yeah!' I said trying to sound as cool as he did as I gulped with difficulty.

'The meeting is in twenty minutes. Give me ten to go through the PPT. OK?' he said as a parting shot in the most casual manner possible.

I sat on my desk for a couple of seconds just concentrating on breathing. The weird channels on tv with semi-naked men doing yoga apparently claim that concentrating on breathing helps one calm down. It did not work. With twenty minutes to go for the meeting, he was now starting work on it? No, correction. He had now asked *me* to work on it. He has no plans whatsoever of doing any work on the PPT himself.

I gulped.

I launched myself into emergency mode and hunted down a PPT that contained the market entrants slide for this year, changed the dates everywhere in last year's marketing strategy PPT, altered the background and looked with dismay at the final product. It was shabby and made little or no sense to say the least. This is what my boss was going to present to the CEO and the marketing head?

I mailed the PPT to Rajeev sir and immediately got a 'Thanks a ton, Kas' reply.

Kas.

I giggled to myself.

A few minutes later I got another mail from him that read as follows:

Hi Kasturi,
In case you do not have prior engagements could you please come for the meeting as well?
Regards,
Rajeev.

I gulped yet again. I did not want to witness the demise of a man's career but Rajeev sir knew how totally empty my diary for the day was. Hence, however unwillingly, I did, a couple of minutes later, made way to the dreaded CEO's cabin. As I seated myself in the farthest corner possible, I saw Rajeev sir walk in looking confident and self assured.

I was introduced to the CEO by Rajeev sir.

'This is Kasturi, management trainee working with me, Lakhan sir. She has made a considerable contribution to the PPT that I am going to present now,' he said. I got up and shook hands with the great, smelly LSD. Fantastic, so now I will witness the slow demise of my own career?

'So, good morning, everyone,' said Rajeev sir confidently as he opened the first slide of the PPT.

I crossed my fingers.

'After the fantastic year we have had, it is now time to start thinking about the future. How do we repeat the same success? Is it going to be difficult? Very difficult? Or...umm...maybe easy?

The strategy has been designed, gentlemen and let me present it to you!' said the suave gentleman.

My fear turned into amazement as in the next one hour Rajeev Mehrotra spoke from a PPT that was more than a year old. Rajeev read off from the PPT, sometimes added his inputs, spoke very confidently and looked so very well prepared that I was zapped! What was going on?

'All this is of course based on the presumption that market growth rate of 7.03 per cent year on year shall be maintained,' continued Rajeev sir throwing around numbers like there was no tomorrow. LSD and the marketing head nodded their heads intelligently.

'Wait a second, Rajeev, the number for income before tax, is it not the same figure we forecasted for last year?' said LSD looking a little unsure.

Bloody hell! All the numbers on the slide are what were forecasted for *last* year! LSD has caught Rajeev sir red-handed, I thought my heart racing.

'Exactly sir!' exclaimed Rajeev sir looking positively pleased at the comment, 'And a man less experienced than you are could not have spotted the trend. Look at this very important slide, sir, how our sales have increased from last years and how the costs have also gone up. Unfortunately, we are therefore ending up with a similar number as forecasted last year.'

LSD nodded his head sadly.

I looked at LSD and then at Rajeev sir. I could not decide whether it was LSD's stupidity that I should be amazed at or Rajeev sir's street-smartness. The same figure for profit yet 7.03 per cent growth rate. Oh bloody hell.

As he finished with the PPT and the questions that came along with it, the impressed CEO asked Rajeev sir how long it had taken him to devise this exhaustive strategy for the coming year.

'Oh well. Sir, I really can't say...I have been thinking about it for over a month now,' said Rajeev sir modestly, 'but Kasturi and I spent the last one week almost completely concentrating on this bit,' he said airily pointing at me.

'Oh yes yes...fresh MBA blood...you must make her work as hard as you do,' CEO LSD said benevolently. I had to disguise my giggle into a cough.

Rajeev saw through the giggle immediately but played on by patting my back, 'Easy Kasturi, easy,' he crooned as I almost fainted right there. It was, as you would notice, the first time Rajeev sir touched me. My my my!

'Too much work for this meeting is taking a toll on this girl,' Rajeev sir said to LSD, looking at me with pity in his eyes. Twelve minutes. It had taken me twelve minutes and the two were talking about me like concerned parents talk about an over industrious child.

'Well...well...it is so nice to see hard working young people! I think the company is in the right hands,' said LSD, grinning from ear to ear and showing all his teeth, white, yellow, black and missing, '...I think you must take your team out for lunch today...,' he added.

Rajeev sir smiled a charming, suave smile.

'Not today sir, Kasturi and I need to get back to another project...it's time critical...neither of us would like to waste office hours...but if the lady is free Friday evening...,' Rajeev sir's voice trailed off as he looked meaningfully at me.

Was he flirting with me right under the CEO's rather uncomplimentary nose? No, he looked like the perfect employee saying 'no' to time off but there was this undercurrent that I could not ignore.

'Yes, ummm . . . no . . . umm . . . I mean . . . no . . . I mean . . . yes . . . umm . . . yeah . . . will come . . . yea . . . ummm,' I fumbled for an eternity. I suddenly felt very weak in my knees and felt an immediate need to sit down and gulp gallons of water.

CEO LSD and the CMO smiled at each other and walked out. As they stepped out of the door I heard LSD say to the CMO in an undertone, 'Take note of the Mehrotra boy . . . he has potential . . . my nose,' he said wiggling the ugly little thing, 'smells a good employee from a mile.'

I stood frozen, trying to register how Rajeev sir had pulled it all off as he walked past me.

'Sir,' I said calling after him.

'Yes, Kasturi?' he said again raising that one perfect eyebrow. His eyes reminded me of delicious, golden brown honey.

'How did you pull this off?' I asked weakly. He smiled. His dimple showed itself in its full glory.

'Learn this art from me Kasturi, if you think you can . . . If we have a new CEO by next year, I will use the same PPT and he too will ask the CMO to keep an eye out for me,' Rajeev sir stopped for a minute, ' . . . I might just use the same PPT even if LSD remains the CEO and will still be able to pull it off,' he added smirking confidently.

'And the numbers? The growth percentages? The revenue numbers, competitors EBIDTA, you knew all of it?' I asked in spite of myself.

'No, I made it up, on the spot,' he said grinning like a cheeky boy, 'I do not know these numbers, Kasturi, but you know what, neither do they,' he nodded towards the retreating figures of LSD and the CMO as Rajeev sir turned around to glide out of the room.

I was staring at his back and subconsciously admiring it when suddenly he turned around and with his chin touching his chest, eyes looking at me from underneath his eye lashes said, 'See you Friday evening for the team dinner?'

Which girl in this galaxy could even think of saying no to him with his eyelashes, brown eyes, broad chest...

'Yes,' I said shyly.

'I will pick you up. ITC Sheraton. Friday 8 p.m., I will book a table for two,' he said and with these words moved out of the board room leaving me yet again gasping for air.

10 June 2009

2.00 a.m.

Why is everyone complaining about the hot weather? Is not this world a beautiful place? Is not life the most beautiful gift ever? Is not everything rosy? Is not everything lovely?

8.00 a.m.

I hate my mum! I just completely cannot stand her. She called some five minutes ago to:

1. Remind me that I have to meet Pita ji. The two sets of parents have fixed both the date, 14 June, Sunday and the venue, food court of Select City Mall. The venue has been chosen as both sets of parents believe that I will be less likely to fall there.

2. Tell me that I have to meet this other guy, Vishal Vikram! He is the same IIT/ IIM guy who was mum's first IIM catch.

Apparently my phone number has been forwarded to him and he is supposed to contact me very soon. I have now decided to not pick up a call from any unfamiliar number.

3. Rant and rave about dad. Mom says she needs someone with whom she can discuss my marriage problems (yeah! that's what she called it) but dad is organising too many outdoor camps. He would, she said, do better for himself and my wedding by doing fewer of these camps and treating more patients who would actually pay him. After all, we are the girl's side and need many lakhs to arrange for the wedding!

4. Generally give me tips about how to look good, how to walk without falling, etc. when meeting guys for marriage purposes.

11 June 2009

What should I wear for the team dinner with Rajeev sir? Jeans? Dress? Black dress? Little dress? Big dress? Hair? Makeup?

12 June 2009

5.00 a.m.

I am so nervous about tomorrow night. What will happen? What will not?

P.S. Thankfully no call yet from V something V something.

9.00 a.m.

What if I smell bad?

10.00 a.m.

What if he thinks my dress is hideous?

2.00 p.m.

What if he chokes on the food we eat, right there, at ITC?

3.00 p.m.

Who goes for dinner with the boss? Is this even a good idea?

5.00 p.m.

What if he trips and hits his head on a table and dies instantly?

6.00 p.m.

What if I fall again? HELL!

13 June 2009

3.00 a.m.

Dear diary,

I do not have words to describe what a night this has been. Let me start from the start. But, oh dear, where is the start? Does this start with my dress hunt? Or with waiting for Rajeev sir? Or when we entered the hotel, together, like a couple?

I picked up a knee length black dress from one of the rather high-end boutiques. The cut was simple but it fit me beautifully. I also bought black strappy high heels to go with the dress. I spent one hour doing my makeup and another doing my hair which I set in soft curls. Of course, I put in a lot of effort to make sure that I looked effortlessly beautiful. And thankfully, when I looked in the mirror at the end of two hours of hard work I was happy with what I saw. I looked delicate and pretty. My skin glowed with a radiance that I found difficult to ignore.

I think I could fall in love with myself.

Rajeev sir called me around 7.30 p.m. to ask for directions to my house. He had not yet started and I had been ready for some ten minutes by then. By the time he reached my house I had transformed into a hopeless mass of nerves. Going out with my boss suddenly did not seem a good idea. I kept on thinking about all that might happen and it started to freak me out. Ananya was not home and I was thankful that I did not have to hide Rajeev's visit from anyone.

I was nervously twirling my fingers and pacing the dining area when I heard the honk of a car. By the time I came out Rajeev sir was out of his car. As I opened the door and saw him standing next to his shiny black car, bathed in the light from the street lamp, all the doubt, fear, anxiety vanished.

He just looked so super-duper perfect! He was wearing black trousers, a full-sleeved white shirt, had done away with his ear studs and was wearing specs. In short, he looked devastatingly handsome. He had outdone himself! As the fear vanished, so did the self-confidence I had been floating in a few minutes back. I felt extremely plain in comparison to him. Why would he want to take *me* out for dinner at ITC?

'For you,' he said with a smile as he handed me the lone red rose he held in his hands, 'you look beautiful,' he said softly, looking intently at my face.

'Thank you, sir,' I said taking the first red rose anyone had ever given me. I just could not look up – almost as if my eye lids were too heavy! I had to then remind myself that I am not the proverbial *gaon ki gori* and I must behave like the B.Tech, MBA girl of the twenty-first century that I am.

'Call me Rajeev, I insist,' he said, 'this is not office and there is nothing remotely official about this dinner,' he said his eyes boring into mine.

I blushed tomato red at this. I don't know why he always has this effect on me. He led me to the car and insisted I wear my seat belt immediately.

'Ohhh, you don't want to pay the hundred rupee fine if we are caught without a seat belt?' I teased him.

He looked at me with a confused look on his face.

'No. What makes you think I would bother about a hundred rupee note? I am just concerned about your safety,' he said. The look on his face shushed me for some minutes. His response had oddly warmed my heart. I grinned like an idiot for the next ten minutes.

The drive to ITC seemed like the tiniest drive ever. The easy banter between us continued. We spoke primarily about office discussing LSD and the CMO and laughing our heads off about the marketing strategy meeting. We randomly discussed cars that whizzed past us, spoke about our mutual love for Delhi, hotly debated the value of Balajee tele serials and what not... Taking cue from Pita ji I actually timed the drive; it took us exactly one hour fifteen minutes. Then why did the drive seem to last just for a few seconds?

As I walked inside the hallowed portals of the ITC (of course, my first time there) still a little unsure in the unfamiliar surroundings, I could see all eyes on us. I caught our reflection in a mirror.

He – tall, well built and a gentleman.

She – delicate, pretty and beautiful.

Together – the perfect couple.

Sigh

The dinner was perfect. There are a million gazillion little things that made the evening with him very special. But I don't remember anything now. And yet I remember everything about the nothing that happened! I want to document each moment of the dinner, of how we made fun of the fat uncle sitting nearby, of how Rajeev refused to talk about office when we were in ITC, of how he kept on asking about me, my family, my likes, my dislikes, of how he listened to each word that came out my mouth, of how he looked at me when I spoke, of how important he made me feel, of how beautiful he made me feel, of how his eyes wandered to my bracelet, of how he shifted his chair closer to mine, of how he told me he thought I was the prettiest girl in the room and of how he did not know where to look when he realised what he had said, of how he remained quiet for the next three to four minutes after that.

Towards the end of our meal, the waiter came to us with some fortune cookies.

'Ladies first,' Rajeev said gallantly.

'No, I want to have a look at yours first,' I insisted as Rajeev indulgently relented and handed his cookie to me.

I cracked open Rajeev's cookie and read out the four words that made me blush once more. If I had a penny for each time I had blushed this evening, I would be, like they say, a millionaire.

'What does it say?' Rajeev insisted.

'Will find love soon,' I read out in a whisper.

Rajeev smiled but kept on looking intently at me. I squirmed under his intent gaze.

'Open yours,' he said to me.

I cracked mine and stared for some seconds at the words in front of me not believing what I was seeing! Four words again. I looked up as my eyes found his.

'What does it say?' Rajeev asked me.

'Will find love soon,' I read from the thin strip of paper in my hands amazed at the coincidence.

I looked up at Rajeev sir. He was resting one elbow on the table and held his chin in one hand. His eyes were looking so intently into mine that I quickly looked elsewhere.

'That's a funny co incidence, *hai na*?' he asked me.

'Yes it is,' I said quietly.

Both of us looked at each other and smiled. In that moment for the first time, I felt truly scared. The spell was broken as the waiter came to us with the bill. I managed to peek in, it read ₹ 3,345. Why was he spending so much on me? Why the rose? Why ITC when a quick Mc Donald's burger would have done the trick? Why make this so special for someone who works as your subordinate in office? These thoughts muddled my head on the way back. He maintained the perfect gentleman's distance from me at all times. To be honest, I was a little disappointed and spent the last half an hour with him in the car on the way back trying to brush my hands against his. He drove well. Not too fast. Not too slow. The perfect speed. He made sure I had the seat belt around me, and fretted excessively about whether the temperature in the car was comfortable for me, if I wanted to change the music, etc. The one hour car drive back home was mostly quiet apart from all this. I was a little tired but content. I felt safe. And content.

The car came to a halt. I could see my house right in front of me. I got out of the car. Rajeev was in front of me.

'Time to say good bye,' Rajeev said.

'Yes,' I said stupidly.

'Well…bye then,' he said not knowing what else to say.

'Bye. Good night,' I replied like an exceptionally dumb girl.

He smiled. His dimple. His lovely dimple. Perfect white teeth. Dark brown eyes. Ears without diamond studs.

'Good night. Get in your house, I will get going once you are inside,' he said.

'Awwwww,' I said mentally.

I walked to my house, opened the door and looked back at him.

He waved. I waved back and closed the door. And as I turned around I was the happiest girl on the planet. I have never felt this way before. Till now Rajeev was just a crush. Like the millions I have had before but now...maybe...just maybe...he might end up being a lot more.

I am just so so HAPPY! Wow! Life is just so beautiful!? Ain't it?

7

Disappearing Act

14 June 2009

3.00 p.m.

Has anyone ever died of happiness? Or will I be the first one?

Rajeev added me on Facebook. According to Facebook, Rajeev Mehrotra had a lovely Saturday evening.

Swoon

There are twelve comments mainly from girls asking him the why, the how, the where and the with whom. Rajeev sir, in his replies is being very mysterious. And I have not stopped smiling since I read the status.

5.00 p.m.

Bloody hell. Mum called me up a few minutes ago. Not even a polite 'hello'.

'Beta, are you on your way? Where have you reached?' she shrieked into the phone.

'I am fine ma, how are you?' I asked pointedly, ready to forgive ma not just for this small yet significant breach of protocol but also for all that she has inflicted upon me over the twenty something years I have existed on this planet.

'Shut up! Where are you?' Ma snapped back.

How rude!

'Why?'

'Because Amay has been waiting for you at Select City for the last fifteen minutes! He called up his mom who called me up instead!' said ma not very happy that potential mother-in-law had called to complain.

OH MY GOD!!!

'I am almost there Ma,' I replied madly and put the phone down. I immediately called up Ananya who was out and not at home.

'Babe, S.O.S,' I said panting for no reason.

'Sure, tell me?' chirped Ananya who, in comparison to me, seemed very happy. Anyone who did not have my mother for a mom would be happy.

'You remember Pita ji?'

'Gaping idiot Pita ji?' asked the intelligent Ananya. You don't get through a top B-school without having at least some brains!

'Bang on! You remember I had asked you for some help?' I quizzed.

'Yes, I am supposed to go with you whenever you have to meet him next,' she said rapidly. She had flexed her muscles threateningly when she had agreed to come with me to meet Pita ji. The flexing of the muscles had been oddly comforting.

'Bingo again.'

I said, 'Now answer this, lady, when was this "whenever" supposed to be?'

'On the fourteenth, 5 p.m.,' she said.

'And today is…' I let it be for effect.

'Oh my gosh!!!!!!' she screamed , 'We are late!'

'Yes' I agreed 'we should have been there fifteen minutes ago,' I added.

'So?' said Ananya.

'So what? Stop doing whatever it is that you are doing! Meet me at Select City!' I ordered.

Thankfully neither of us was too far from the meeting spot. I threw on a pair of jeans and the first top I could find that was neither stinking nor torn and dashed out of the house. My mom would kill me. No kidding, she will, if she ever found out!

Thirty-five minutes later, Ananya and I found each other at the entrance of Select City Mall. I called up gaping idiot Pita ji.

'Hi Pita…errr…Amay.' I said.

'Hi Kasturi.' I could *hear* his idiotic frown.

'Hey, where are you? I have been waiting for you for the last twenty minutes,' I said. Aggression is the best form of defense. What then followed was a successful attempt at thoroughly confusing poor Pita ji. Ananya kept grimacing next to me as I played with Pita ji's precious head.

Finally, after some haggling we figured out a common place to meet. We made our way to the food court and soon saw Pita ji approach us.

'Hi Amay.' I said.

'Hi Kasturi.' I could now *see* his frown. Haah! I already knew him so well!

'This is my friend, Ananya. Ananya, Amay. Amay, Ananya.' I did the introductions.

Pita ji looked confused. Two two girls! His pea-sized brain would have imploded. But I was not going to meet Pita ji alone after what had happened last time! The three of us sat down and silence reigned supreme. I was, however, hardly bothered with the niceties. Also, I had no intentions of starting or participating in any form of conversation. I therefore, soon busied myself with the all important task of thinking about Rajeev sir and how perfect the dinner had been.

Rajeev's face kept coming back to me again and again. Endlessly. I wondered if this was love. I shuddered at the thought when a strange eerie feeling enveloped me. What if I really fell in love? What then? I am no longer in that age and stage where I can have a couple of romances. Where would it all head? Why was Rajeev Sir showing so much interest in me. I am not pretty enough, I am not cool enough and I am not rich enough. Why then? Something was not adding up but I felt too consumed by the attention to bother.

My thoughts were broken by the sound of helpless peals of laughter that seemed to originate from somewhere disturbingly close. I turned around to see Ananya laughing hysterically and Pita ji looking smug having probably made the first successful joke of his miserable life which so far had primarily been spent gaping at girls who had tripped and fallen. I lazily noted that I had never seen Anu laugh like this. She almost looked like a girl!

'You really said that!' exclaimed Ananya, looking absolutely incredulous.

Pita ji nodded his head so vigorously that I was scared it would bounce right off his shoulders. I had the macabre vision of Pita ji's head near the foot of the table and a headless Pita ji in front of me. The perverse me stifled a giggle.

'Wow,' said Ananya looking incredulous at how anyone could be so adventurous with words. I left the two of them and went back to my thoughts. Coffee came and went. When I had thought enough about Rajeev sir and there was little more to think about, I came out of my trance.

Ananya and Pita ji were still immersed in their animated discussion. This had been such a big help – getting Ananya with me. I could not have dealt with Pita ji for one second today with thoughts of Rajeev all over in my head.

'I think it is time to get going,' I said after observing them for a few minutes.

'Yeah, let's get going,' said Ananya, smiling.

We soon parted ways with Pita ji looking most reluctant to let us go. When I reached home, the first thing I did was to call up ma to tell her that Pita ji and I were not a possibility.

'Since when have you started calling dad Pita ji? And what possibility is there between you and dad?' questioned my mom, very confused.

'Mom, I mean Amay. I don't like him. I won't meet him anymore,' I said flatly.

'Why?' mum wailed.

'Because I do not like him. I do not want to meet him at all,' I stood firm.

'Oh...OK,' said mom sadly but seeming to agree anyways. I immediately felt suspicious.

'Then there is this other guy you need to meet. He is a doctor and I have fixed the meeting for next weekend,' my mother said.

What!! Was there going to be a new guy each weekend? And this is why she did not raise hell when I said I did not want to meet Pita ji again. I know my mom so very well, I thought grimly as I braced myself to start protesting against any further meetings with doctors/ engineers/ prime ministers.

15 June 2009

8.00 a.m.

In my excitement of meeting Rajeev I have reached office one and a half hours early. There are some guys in rather cute blue overalls, sweeping the floor. I even helped one of the cuter ones by moving around chairs as he swept the floor.

9.30 a.m.

No sign of Rajeev sir. I have already peeped into his cabin five times and have walked past it seven times.

10.30 a.m.

I have walked past his cabin eleven times in the last one hour. No sign of Rajeev sir. Maybe he is in a board meeting.

12.00 p.m.

No sign of Rajeev. No updates on Facebook either. Where is he?

2.00 p.m.

Received a text from Rajeev.

> *Stuck in Chandigarh. Will take two days. Can you email me the PPT you were supposed to make today. I need to speak to the Chandigarh head here. Thanks.*

I felt weird reading the text though I could not zero in on the exact reason. I was hoping for at least one smiley in the text or maybe even an 'I miss you'. Or something a little more personal. Something that would associate with our evening together.

Something, anything. There was nothing of that sort. Not a single smiley. Not a single 'I miss you'. I checked my phone thirty-one times for a text from him.

16 June 2009

Office seems like a dreary place without Rajeev sir. Yes, I have gone back to calling him sir. After all if he sends me such professional texts then I should speak professionally to and about him? Right? In fact I do not think I am speaking to him at all now. I made it a point to not reply to the text. I just mailed him the PPT from my office email id. This was the mail I sent.

> *Dear sir,*
> *PFA the PPT requested on text.*
> *Thanks and Regards,*
> *Kasturi Shukla.*

I hope he spends the rest of his life hunting for smileys in mails that he gets. Let the curse of mails without smileys fall unto him.

Huh!

I checked my phone twenty-seven times and my email thirteen times today for some message from him.

8

Number Two

17 June 2009

Mum called to inform me of a change in her grand plans. It is, I realised today, absolutely amazing that she lives some thousand kilometers away from where I live and is still able to micro-manage and micro-control every big, small aspect of my life. Apparently, guy no.2 wants to meet me tomorrow and not on Saturday as previously planned because he has to attend some conference then. I said yes for the meeting for two reasons. First, because I am very angry at Rajeev for not even calling/ mailing/ texting me since our dinner date. And second because, I think mum would have anyways forced me into it.

I checked my phone forty-one times today for a missed call/ call/ message/ missed message from Rajeev sir. This has been my highest count so far. I have to stop obsessing.

Or stop counting.

18 June 2009

Guy no.2 is officially called Dr Purva Dikshit. He is currently doing his super specialisation in cardio·thoracic surgery at the prestigious AIMMS College. He could have failed his class twelfth boards, not studied any further and spent years loitering around ogling at girls in his village and I would have happily agreed to meet him. Such was my anger at Rajeev Sir and his unexplained absence. After a quick exchange of emails, Purva and I decided to meet at Dilli Haat.

To take my mind off Rajeev sir, I concentrated on getting ready. I wore a pink and blue salwar-kurta, put on some lip gloss, hunted out an old kajal pencil and outlined my eyes. I found some matching long earrings and as a final touch to the Indian ensemble I put on lovely silver bangles. Ananya who was sitting on my bed typing furiously on her laptop occasionally looked up at me and grimaced as she saw me apply layer after layer of makeup. Her distaste was obvious and not at all encouraging. As I studied myself in the mirror the phone rang.

'Hi, may I please speak to Ms Kasturi Shukla,' a nice voice said.

'This is Kasturi,' I desperately hoping that the voice belonged to Rajeev Sir.

'Oh, hi Kasturi, this is Purva. I guess your mum or dad would have spoken to you about me,' he said.

'Yes, they have indeed,' I agreed.

'Great! So I will see you in half an hour at Dilli Haat? I just thought I will confirm,' the nice voice asked.

'Sure.'

'Bye.'

'Bye.'

And with that the conversation ended. I have to say that no. 2 has a nice voice. Though I cannot say I am looking forward to meeting him, I am getting this feeling that he might not be *that* bad after all. Only thing is I need to make sure that I do not fall flat on my face.

Yet again.

I checked my phone eighteen times today. The count is low and I am proud of that.

19 June 2009

So, I am back from my date with Dr Purva Dikshit. Purva, brooding, serious Purva! The shops and the colourful items displayed were, beyond any doubt, infinitely more interesting.

But now, after analysing, reanalysing and re-reanalysing each big/small detail on the phone with Varun, I must say I had quite an OK time with him mainly because conversing with him was quite easy. It was one-sided, no doubt, with me doing all the talking but he listened patiently. He walked with me from shop to shop and did not mind it if I lingered too long at any one of them.

Purva is certainly not very good looking and really nothing in comparison to Rajeev sir, obviously, but he is definitely nice looking in a quiet, sensible way. He is 5'10 (yes, I asked), is very fair with dark black eyes. His features are plain but there is a calmness and intelligence on his face that I found appealing when I saw him first. He was dressed casually in jeans and a blue shirt that seemed to go well with the 'I-am-a-very-serious-doctor' look that he had on his face all throughout the evening.

'I am done with window shopping,' I announced after about half an hour. Dusk had fallen and yellow bulbs in colourful lamps had been lit everywhere making the place look all the more surreal and beautiful. People were milling about, shopping, eating and laughing.

'You could not have done it at all' Purva said.

'Why?' I asked genuinely interested.

'There are no windows in most of these shops!' he chuckled.

Duh-uh!

'I could crack better PJs than this even before I could speak,' I said laughing in spite of the lameness of the PJ. He grinned.

'I am hungry,' I announced after sometime eyeing a Chinese food stall.

'Let's eat, then,' was Purva's intelligent reply.

'I will let you decide the stall. Let us see what your doctor brain comes up with this time,' I teased. I stopped short suddenly. There is no need to be so overtly friendly with him, I told myself very strictly. Purva chose the Rajasthani stall. We were waiting for the food to arrive when light fell on his face and I noticed a tiny scar near his eyes.

Not that I remember, but have I ever spoken to you of my fascination with scars? Point to be noted is that I do not have a single scar on the length/breadth of my body. And you know what is a funnier, bordering on bizarre fact?

Till a few days back I had never had the sad experience of falling down. No, not even once. There is always a first time but that first time really did not need to be in a crowded restaurant in front of an idiotic man who has no manners. I cringed again at the memory. Life could definitely be very unfair at times. I let out a melodramatic sigh.

'How did you get this?' I asked Purva pointing to his scar.

'In a fire,' was his three word reply as he gingerly touched the scar and grimaced most probably at the memory.

'What fire?' I prodded further.

'House-fire.'

'So who saved you?'

'No one.'

'Then how did you come out?'

'I had gone in for someone, so I came out on my own.' he said.

'And...,' I asked further.

'Nothing.'

'What nothing?' I asked now irritated, '...you got the person out, didn't you?'

'No.' he said.

'What "No"' I said, laughing.

I stopped short as the meaning sunk in.

'You mean you could not save the person you had gone in for,' I asked looking at him gravely. The conversation had taken an abrupt turn.

'No, I could not,' he said looking at the tattered menu very closely.

The moon that had been shining on his face hid behind some clouds and I could no longer see his expression. But his voice sounded heavier. A million questions propped in my head.

'You like Rajasthani food?' he asked smiling, changing the topic as the moon shone on his face once again. The waiter had brought in delicious looking food.

As thick skinned as I generally am, I understood that I should not prod further. I will not meet him again anyways so how does it matter, I reasoned with myself? I would have liked to know more, though.

'It's yummm!' I said comically smacking my lips trying to make him smile. He laughed.

After the lovely dinner, we strolled around for some more time talking about random things in life. He told me stories about AIMMS, about his family, about his best friend Ajay, who is also a doctor at AIMMS. I, in turn, spent over an hour giving him an in-depth description of LSD's denture. Before we knew it was 10.00 p.m. and time to say good bye, which we did soon enough. As I returned home, I realised that we had not spoken one word about the potential marriage. I kind of liked that.

However the best thing about time spent with Purva was that it had helped me keep my mind off Rajeev sir. Throughout the day, I checked my phone for a text/call from Rajeev just fourteen times, an exceptionally low number. However, I checked gmail for a mail from him thirty-four times though most of it was done once I came back home after meeting Purva.

Why has he not called or mailed? Why?

9

V-something V-something from IIM-A

20 June 2009

I hate Saturdays because that's when my mum knows I am free
and talks to me for hours on the phone. Correction. She talks to
me for hours about the boy hunt and how she has the huge-est
possible list of boys all of whom I should meet at the earliest.
As with each of her conversations of late, she dropped another
bomb in this one!

'Beta,' ma said sweetly. I was immediately suspicious. Once
bitten twice shy.

'Yes mom,' said I crossing my fingers.

'Beta, so how did it go with Purva, Beta?' Too many 'betas'
in one sentence for my comfort.

'It was OK' I said dryly hoping that the tone of my voice
would put her off.

'When are you meeting him next?' said mum too thick
skinned to be bothered by something as trivial as the tone of
her daughter's voice.

'I do not know.'

'Not any time soon?'

'Not that I know,' I said unwilling to commit either ways.

'Good, that means you are free this week!' she exclaimed with fake happiness.

'Yes.' I said.

'Great! You remember Vishal Vikram whom I told you about?' she said chattily.

Sigh! I was hoping mum had forgotten about the IIM-A guy! Since IIM-A is the best B-school in the country, he is the best possible bachelor one can get by way of an arranged marriage. This explained Mum's sudden loss of interest in Purva. He is, after all, just a doctor.

'No.' I lied.

'*Arre* beta, the IIM-A guy, nice little mole on the lip?' Mum said helpfully.

Little?

And more importantly 'nice'? That disgusting looking thing! What was wrong with mum?

'Ohhh...yess...I don't think I will be able to stand him for a second,' I said flatly in a stern voice.

'Beta!' Mum said disapprovingly. I instinctively knew what would come next.

'Beta, he is from IIM-A and works with such a big company! He must be very intelligent to have cracked all these big exams. On top of that he has done his B.Tech from IIT K! If he is not the perfect boy for you who would be? Imagine, beta, how intelligent your kids will be!' she finished with a triumphant flourish.

I felt too exhausted from thinking about Rajeev to bother about Vishal Vikram and our hypothetical future kids.

'Fine, I will meet him,' I said dryly.

'Good. Tomorrow then? Pizza Hut?' said mum, as usual, all set with the details even before I had finished saying 'yes'. I sighed a deep, sad sigh.

'Yes. Just give me the time by tonight,' I said to her.

21 June 2009

I finally met Vipul Vikas or whatever his name is today. And I have just one tiny question I need an immediate answer to. Why do I have to go through this nonsense? Why, god, why? Anu's folks are not forcing her into meeting boys then why are mine?

Anyways, I reached Pizza Hut a little early and was fiddling with the menu when Vishal Vikram walked in. It was difficult to miss him. He was taller than I had imagined – over six easily, very thin, quite dark and with that HUGE mole right above his lips.

'Hi,' he said extending his hand.

I already felt tired of the whole nonsense of meeting a new boy each nanosecond.

'Hi,' I said dryly.

We sat down and he stared fixedly at my face. Alarmed, I felt all over my face rather frantically. Had another zit popped up somewhere without my knowledge? Or were there any bits of food on my face?

'So what do you think of marriage?' he asked me his first question that came a second later while I was engrossed in checking my face for zits and bits of food.

'I think nothing about marriage,' was my purposely stupid answer. I was hoping the IIM-A guy would be put off by stupid answers.

'Very nice,' he seemed quite pleased with my answer. With that he fixed his gaze some inches below my chin. AAARRRGGGHH!

'What are your views on Indo-Pak relations?' came his second question.

I mean like what?!

'I am sorry,' I said politely, quite sure I had heard him wrong.

'Your views on Indo-Pak relations?' he repeated himself patiently.

'And you ask me this because...,' I asked with a smile hoping that would disguise my horror.

'Because I hold very strong views on the issue and I need to see if yours match mine,' he explained patiently.

Women do not admit their age. Men don't act theirs.

'Oh, of course,' I said as if his explanation made it all logical. This guy cannot be in his right mind, I thought to myself.

'But what if I do not have a view on the issue?' I asked him bending forward and speaking in a grave almost sinister whisper. I tried to look as if I was waiting for his reply with baited breath. He looked grave and seemed to ponder for a few minutes.

'I do not know then...about us... "we" might never happen,' was his final answer after due deliberation.

'Ahhhhh,' I said fully understanding the gravity of the situation. I drew back.

Right then the waiter came to take our order. My interrogation was stopped for a few minutes. Vikram Vipul seemed very irritated with the disturbance.

'Did you read the newspaper today?' asked Vikas Vikram as soon as the waiter left.

'Yes,' I said. I resisted the temptation of adding 'sir'.

'Can you tell me the headlines?' he asked. While waiting for my response, he took out a small black notebook and a pen. It seemed worn-out and quite a few pages were filled in a painfully neat handwriting. He seemed ready to write down something.

'You want the headlines?' I asked raising my eyebrows. Surely I had heard wrong.

'Yes,' he said primly pushing spectacles up his nose and looking expectantly at me. His mole quivered. It seemed to have a life of it's own. It moved and swayed.

'Aaaha,' I said and tried to breathe again. Not breathing is not really good for health, I reminded myself as I gave him the headlines stammering quite a bit in between. I chuckled to myself once I was done. Seeing him tick something in his book, I peeped over a little bit to see what he was writing. This is what I saw in the diary:

Name: Kasturi Shukla
Caste, Education: Brahmin, MBA
Location of the meeting: Pizza Hut
Date and Time of meeting: 21 June 2009, 6.30 p.m.
Knowledge about current affairs: Sketchy but OK

I read the last line with indignation. Sketchy? I spend at least one hour with the newspaper each day and read every possible thing! Sketchy? Hmmpff!

He then underlined my name a couple of times and scribbled industriously for the next few minutes. I waited patiently for him to finish documenting whatever it was that he found worth documenting. Wow!

'I am sorry for asking you this but how many, if any, boyfriends have you had in the past?' he asked pen in hand, pushing up his spectacles and looking up from the notes he had been making.

'None,' I said too stunned to not answer.

He raised one eyebrow in disbelief. His breathing quickened. He gazed at my left breast for some seconds. Then he ticked something in his notebook.

'Not even one in B-school?' his mole danced on his lip as his breathing became heavier.

'No,' I said now amused.

'Very nice,' he said and started scribbling furiously. With a victorious smile on his lips, Varun Vipul continued to scribble for an eternity. He then spent a long time underlining some bits of what he had just written and it was only after neatly folding a little bit of the top right bit of the page that he shut his note book. He seemed oddly victorious; he had found what he had been looking for for a long time now. That freaked me out. He just would not stop grinning. His upper lip would quiver making his mole do the dance.

When I had had enough of the dancing mole, I politely told him that it was time for me to go. Vikram Vijay did not stop grinning till we parted ways. The moment I set eyes on his thin narrow back, I called up dad and told him, in all seriousness, that I will jump into the Yamuna if Vikram Vishal's name is ever mentioned in front of me.

Dad was kind enough to point out two things to me:

1. Boy's name is not Vikram Vishal. His correct full name continues to be a mystery.

2. The Yamuna water is very dirty and stinks so much that my last few minutes on earth will not be very pleasant should I take that route to end my life. Dad was also helpful enough to point out that there are many other more comfortable ways of accomplishing the same objective.

Though, for all practical purposes I hope I have seen the last of Vikram Vijay and his great mole, this meeting has left an indelible mark on my innocent and so far uncorrupted mind, heart and soul.

10

Scene toh Poora Filmy hai, Friendship Mein no Sorry, no Thank You!

22 June 2009

With too much going on in my head to sleep for the regular twelve hours, I reached office at the unearthly hour of nine in the morning. I had not yet stepped inside when my heart skipped a couple of thousand beats and I felt my BP shoot up like a space shuttle being fired into outer space.

The reason for these extreme physiological changes was the fact that my eyes had just caught sight of Rajeev sir walking from one cubicle to another. He was back! He was all right! He had not been killed/murdered/kidnapped! He was back, in one piece. One lovely, beautiful piece. I could not breathe for a few minutes. Why? Why does he have this affect on me? Why? I felt strangely captive of my own emotions.

I could not let him, no correction, I could not let anyone see me right then and hence I, in a movement as quick as that of a detective in a cheap Hindi movie, turned to my right to seek solace in the ladies room to gather my wits. I felt miserably weak.

I stood in front of the huge mirror. Black trousers, my favourite pink shirt as usual tucked in and my hair straightened. I looked so confident on the outside and was such an entangled mess of nerves on the inside simply because I had spotted, after one week, a guy with whom I had gone out for one single dinner.

One single heavenly dinner. I sighed.

I sat on the bathroom floor for some time as my heart started beating again, my BP normalised and I started breathing again. Overcome with anger, I felt like rolling up some toilet paper and thwacking Rajeev's head with it.

Used toilet paper.

Feeling much better after thinking visually about used toilet paper around his head, I came out of my hideout and headed towards my desk distributing cheerful and confident hellos and good mornings to the few people who had managed to reach office at this early and unearthly an hour. I had decided to give Rajeev the cold shoulder and was dutifully checking Facebook for the nth time for any interesting updates when he appeared at my desk some forty minutes later.

'Hi,' he said quietly.

I quickly alt+tab-ed to the company website. 'Yes Sir,' I said very professionally.

'Are you mad at me?' he asked in a forced whisper with his brow furrowing. The diamond stud was missing and he was unshaved which made him look doubly sexy. Seriously!

'I am sorry sir, I hope you got the PPT in time for your meeting,' I replied continuing to use the professional tone.

'Listen I am really sorry. I know I should have called. But at least hear me out!' he pleaded in whisper. I continued to look at him with the proverbial daggers in my eyes.

'Are you angry?' he asked again.

'No sir,' I replied diverting my gaze once I had given him a very dirty look. While doing these theatrics I was actually pleasantly surprised by how apologetic Rajeev sir seemed. I was not even sure I had any right to be angry in the first place. After all we had just one dinner together, nothing more.

'Please look at me,' he whispered. I stubbornly refused to look at him.

'Listen, can you meet me outside for lunch?' he pleaded again in a hushed whisper. From the corner of my eye I saw Varun looking closely at us.

'No, I am sorry I have to go for a meeting with the CMO,' I said as I scooped my laptop and glided out of sight.

Correction.

I *would* have glided out of his sight in one elegant movement had I remembered to yank off the power cable of the laptop. I had not taken two swift steps when my laptop *almost* fell off my hands, three files fell to the ground and in all my haughtiness I had to stoop to the level of taking Rajeev's help. I could not refuse, everyone in office was staring at us and I did not wish to create a scene in front of everybody.

What has happened to me! Have I forgotten to walk? Do my parents need to teach me how to walk once again. I felt like crying.

4.00 p.m.

Text from Rajeev sir:

'I am sorry. Please talk to me, please please ☹'

I chose to not reply.

6.00 p.m.

I finished work at around 4.30 p.m. today but have been pretending to be hard at work since. Rajeev sir has tried speaking to me thrice but I feel too angry to respond to him. Yet I am faking work, just to be around him.

Sigh

Love

11.00 p.m.

There are eleven missed calls from Rajeev.

My cell has not been away from me for even a single second today. And god knows I have waited like crazy for each of these calls. Also god alone knows how much satisfaction I have gained out of not picking any of those calls. I feel content and happy now that I have his undivided attention.

To make matters worse for him and also to teach him a lesson, I am planning to take sick leave from office tomorrow.

Given the ease with which I can concoct such devious plans, I think I should be the one writing the script of those *saas bahu* serials. Seriously.

23 June 2009

8.00 a.m.

I should ideally call up Rajeev as he is my boss and tell him that I have fever (which, as you know, I do not). But just to spite and hopefully pain Rajeev I called up the CMO.

'*Cough* *Cough*'

'Hello? Hello? I cannot hear you. Who is it? Hello? Hello,' repeated the CMO.

'Oh hello sir, this is Kasturi, sir,' I said in what I believed to be the pitiful, trembling voice of someone down with high fever.

'Yes Kasturi, why such an early call? Are you ok?' asked the concerned manager.

'Not really sir. I am not well. I think I have very high fever sir,' I said in a voice that sounded horribly fake to me.

'Oh no!' said the CMO proving once again that having grey cells was not a criteria essential to climb the proverbial corporate ladder.

'I need to take the day off, sir.' I said.

'You will have to call up Rajeev, Kasturi, you report to him,' the CMO was kind enough to remind me.

'Yes sir, I know that sir, but I am not able to reach him. I have been trying to get in touch with him for a long time now,' I lied.

For some extra effect I pretended to sound like I was having trouble breathing.

'There is some disturbance in the line,' said the manager.

'No sir, it is okay,' I reassured the CMO who I realised, has no eye or ear for a theatrical performance.

'Okay, I will tell Rajeev that you won't be coming to office today. Do take care of your health,' he said kindly.

'Yes sir, I will,' I promised him. I coughed a few fake coughs just for the effect, the CMO sighed and we both cut the line.

Maybe I should think about acting as an alternate career?

10.30 p.m.

I had just come out of the shower at around six in the evening, taken out a huge box of chocolate ice cream from the refrigerator and was checking my cell for any more concerned texts from Rajeev when the door bell rang.

For the record, I have received a deluge of frantic texts from Rajeev (thirty-seven in total!). He seems deeply concerned and has been (as he should) blaming himself for my (supposed) ill-health. I have, obviously, chosen to not reply to his messages. I, however, did send him a one-liner telling him that I was too ill to get out of bed and that the doctor had blamed my state on mental stress which has led to a weakened immune system. I have, of course, not picked up even one of his twenty-one calls.

Life, really, is not so bad after all.

Anyways, coming back to the door bell, with my hair all wet, dressed in obnoxiously tiny shorts, ice cream in hand, spring in the step and twisting my body to the sound of '*Ishq Kamina*' blaring in the back ground, I opened the door.

I opened the door and stood there not able to move an inch of my body for what seemed like an eternity.

In front of me was none other than Rajeev sir. In one hand he carried a huge bouquet of flowers and in the other he carried three or four big plastic bags. His expression changed from deep concern to equally deep surprise and then to equally deep anger in a matter of seconds after his angry eyes fell on me.

'Kas...,' he tried to take my name but faltered mid way out of sheer disbelief and anger.

'Hi,' I did not know where to look. Would the *dharti* please part and take me in?

'You...you...you...don't have fever?' he asked incredulous, stammering a little bit.

'No no, I do,' I said and gave one fake cough.

'That's fake!' he exclaimed.

'No it is not!' I exclaimed.

'You are absolutely fine!' he said indignantly

'No, I am not!' I said equally indignantly.

'Of course you are! Look at your face, its glowing like there are some three hundred light bulbs under your skin! Your eyes, they are shining like licked, black stones! Your body language, absolutely healthy! Your hands, you...you...have one huge box of ice cream there!' he spoke nonstop. I could see that the ice cream was a bit too much for him to digest. A weaker man would have succumbed to the pressure and had a heart attack. But not him. He is a man of steel. My respect for the man grew by leaps and bounds.

'Do you know what I am?' he continued belligerently pointing a finger at himself.

'Homosapien?' I tried weakly casting down my eyes.

'An idiot! Spelt as I-D-I-T,' he said passionately.

'You missed the "O",' I muttered under my breath, too meek to speak out loud.

'What? What are you muttering under your breath?' he thundered, 'Do you have any idea how concerned I have been about you! The CMO told me that you were very ill and were not even able to breathe! Do you know what that did to me? Do you know I cancelled three meetings to come and see you? Do you have any idea at all about how guilty I have been feeling all this while?'

I looked down at my feet feeling miserable when my eyes fell on the plastic bags in his hands. He saw my eyes straying towards the packets in his hands.

'Do you know why I am an idiot?' he asked.

'No,' I replied meekly.

He glared at me for a second, held me by the elbow and pulled me inside the house. There he emptied the three packets on my bed.

'Medicine box, and because I did not know which medicines you already had, I got *all* of them. ALL,' he said picking up the huge packet of medicines and throwing it back on the bed again. There were enough medicines in there for the whole of Africa.

'See all this,' he took out ten packets of juice, fruits and some chocolates. With each item he took out of the bag, my heart sank further.

'And look at my phone,' he navigated to the dialled calls section. All I could see was 'Kasturi-Office'.

My heart sank further. I felt really small and wished I was amongst the lucky ones who could disappear when they wanted to.

'How many Kasturi's do you know?' I ventured bravely once again.

'What?' he looked confused.

'You have stored my number as "Kasturi-office", as if you know a "Kasturi-bath room" and a "Kasturi-kitchen" and a "Kasturi-storeroom",' I said intelligently.

Rajeev glared at me. I lowered my eyes. No more weak jokes to lighten the situation, I ordered myself.

'I am sorry,' I said quietly.

'Why did you lie to me?' he asked me in a voice that did not seem quite as harsh or angry.

'Because I wanted you to feel scared and concerned,' I said honestly.

'Because I did not call you for a few days after our dinner?' he asked gently.

'Seven days,' I said glumly. He smiled and with that the anger seemed to ebb.

'But you didn't even let me explain,' he said softly.

I kept looking down.

'I went to Chandigarh for a day to discuss the deal we were working on, and the next day I was really very busy meeting the head of Chandigarh zone. I was saving all the news and wanted to speak to you only when I knew for sure that we got the order so I did not call. I went home that night ready to get back to work and the project early next day. But, as luck would have it, I spent the whole night with my ill grandmother who had taken a turn for the worse. We rushed her to the hospital early in the morning when things got really bad. They had to do an emergency operation... She is OK now,' he added seeing my horrified expression. I had gasped a couple of times during this monologue.

'There was so much happening...I had no clue what I was doing. I had a miserable time,' he said looking down. My brain buzzed with activity. Of course, this explained his absence. I felt ashamed about all the vile things I had been thinking about.

'Why did you not call and tell me?' I questioned.

'Kasturi, I can ask the same question. Why didn't *you* call me? You sent me one small email. You did not even put a smiley in it, it was so professional. I thought you were angry with me!'

I could not help but smile inwardly when he spoke of the smiley. Haaah!

'Why would I be angry?' I asked surprised.

'You did not call me or text me or email me. You did not try to find out why I was not in office. You did not even speak to me once I got back to office!' he exclaimed and looked quite stricken.

'I was waiting for you to call!' I said.

'Oh my!' he held his head in his hands as it all sunk in. He was waiting for me to call and I was waiting for him to call. This was ridiculous! I started laughing at the absurdity of it all. His furrowed brow eased when he saw me in peals of laughter. In the next few seconds, I saw his face break into a smile that instantly warmed my heart.

'Friends again?' I asked extending my hand in what I thought was a very sweet and filmy gesture.

'Friends,' he agreed smiling as he took my hand.

'Thanks,' I said returning his smile.

'Friendship *mein*...no sorry, no thank you,' he said grinning his goofy grin as my Bollywood crazy and very lovable boss repeated the famous dialogue from *Maine Pyaar Kiya*. And as per tradition older than the movie, I blushed. I think I can blush at anything Rajeev sir says. He might tell me that his cocker spaniel died and I am fully capable of blushing at that as well. That is how pathetic I am around Rajeev sir.

Anyways, so that is how we stood there, in the middle of my room. Rajeev sir and I. In my room. He with that wide smile on his gorgeous face and I with that idiotic blush. We stood like that for a long time. Neither of us wanted the moment to end. And as I looked at Rajeev sir's happy, smiling face, I heaved a sigh of relief, happy with the turn of events. The world was rosy again and I was happy again.

11

Butter and Microwave

24 June 2009

10:00 p.m.

Rajeev and I were both in office and for a change, were on talking terms. We kept stealing glances at each other the whole of today. We exchanged a total of thirty-five messages, thirteen calls (of which ten were related to work) and fourteen missed calls (of which none were related to work).

25 June 2009

Do you remember Purva, the quiet doctor? Well apparently his mother called up my mom. After the initial pleasantries the following happened:

'Behen ji, you should see the number of people running after my son!' exclaimed the doctor's mother seemingly stricken by the number of parents of would-be-brides chasing her one and only.

'Oh behen ji, you should see the number of responses we have got for Kasturi's newspaper ad in *The Times of India*,' retorted my mother not to be outdone in anything.

'Really, that's surprising,' said Purva's Mom.

'What? What do you mean?' demanded my mother the very next instant.

'Well...now...now...that you ask, my son is so fair, your daughter is not really fair, so to say. Quite dark in fact...who would be interested in her?' observed my prospective mother-in-law very thoughtfully. After all a dark girl is a dark girl. And dark skin can be a potential problem when finding a husband. We all have spent enough hours in front of the television, empathising with the dark skinned girl on tv who spends hours crying on her bed because she cannot find a boy who will go beyond the colour of her skin and see her inner beauty.

'Not fair?' shouted my mother, aghast.

I firmly believe that my mother would have gone all theatrical this point onwards. To be fair, I am not exactly the fair and lovely ad girl material. And what's worse, I get my skin colour from dad. Mum is exceptionally fair. This has, therefore, always been a sore spot for mum.

'Well...certainly not fair,' declared potential mum-in-law after due deliberation.

'I think this is very rude,' said Mum

'I am just being honest,' retorted Purva's Mum.

'I am glad you showed your "honest" side to us before the kids decided anything that we could not reverse,' my mother is believed to have said very angrily.

Things, from what I gather, went horribly downhill after this and ended with the two women screaming profanities at each other. The two parties accused one another of a surprisingly large number of things which was quite commendable because the two women had just spoken some three to four times over the phone and not even met once!

Bottom line is that mum is very glad I am not too keen on 'that doctor guy'. She is sure anyone and any family would be ten times better than 'that doctor guy' and his obnoxious family.

Oh well.

Another chapter closes.

25 June 2009

I had just come out after an 8 p.m. after-office-bath and was totally absorbed in cat-walking in front of the mirror while combing my hair when Anu walked in. She seemed dressed. And her top had some glittery things on it. And it was pink! Anu and glittery pink tops so don't go together. I looked at her with immediate suspicion.

'Kas,' said Anu.

I thrust my face at the mirror and jutted out my hips in that perfect sophisticated model strut.

'Yes,' I said in a haughty accented voice turning my face towards Anu in a slow elegant movement.

'Shut up! And straighten up!' Anu snapped impolitely.

'How rude,' I thought to myself as I grimaced and straightened up. Ananya lingered around my mirror which almost covered the entire wall, a rarity. She absently fingered my cosmetics bag kept on the table.

'What is this Kas?' asked Ananya pulling out a lip gloss.

'Lip gloss,' I said once again impressed by Anu's lack of even basic information about basic cosmetics.

'How do you put it on? I mean nicely...without smudging...,' she said looking everywhere except into my eyes. I narrowed my eyes and looked at her. I had not yet properly recovered from her pink and glittery top and she was now coming up with questions about makeup? I felt a little dizzy.

'Are you going somewhere?' I asked, as I pulled out the lip gloss stick and started applying it for her.

'Yeah...just for half an hour...to meet an old friend,' she mumbled as I outlined her mouth using a lip pencil.

I was intelligent enough to not ask any further questions. I-hate-makeup, I-will-never-dress-for-anything-or-anybody Ananya wanted to put on lip gloss. After putting on a top that was pink in colour and had glitter on it. Oh Dear Lord. I need to sit down.

26 June 2009

I have never been so excited about work. Ok, I am not excited about work now either, but I love going to office because that is where I get to meet Rajeev sir.

Sometimes we chat on the office intranet and text each other while sitting in the same meeting. All this is so very exciting!

27 June 2009

11.14 a.m.

Is it possible to jump from your seat and keep sitting as well?

I just got a text from Rajeev Sir:

'Wanna come for a cup of coffee?'

I think I almost fainted.

11.15 a.m.

Should I play hard to get? I think it is imperative that I do. I should not reply to the message for at least the next three hours. He, anyways, knows that I am very busy today. I have to change the background colour of three PPTs and take photocopies of four files.

11.16 a.m.

Replied with a yes!

11.00 p.m.

Rajeev sir and I went for coffee today. We were very secretive and like celebrities who do not wish for the paparazzi to follow, we left the office premises separately. Rajeev sir left before I did but I was already seated and had ordered a Mojita by the time he joined me.

'Hi,' he said smiling as he pulled a chair closer to me.

'Hi again,' I said.

'How is fever?' he chuckled to himself. He has been asking about my health ever since the fever incident. He even inquired about my fever in front of LSD who then went on to give me a long list of medical problems he and his wife have been facing in the last fifty to sixty years they have spent on the planet.

'Much better! A friend got me loads of medicines. They seem to have worked,' I said batting my eye lids.

Rajeev sir looked into my eyes and smiled that extra special smile of his. I felt as if my heart was made of butter. His smile is like a microwave. When the microwave is on, the butter melts.

'What are you thinking of?' Rajeev sir asked looking deep into my eyes.

'Butter,' I said mysteriously.

He threw back his head and laughed a loud laugh. I like it when he laughs at the goofy things I do and say.

'So you mean to say that you really missed me when I was away,' he said out of the blue referring to our conversation from a few days back.

'No! Of course not!' I lied indignantly.

He smiled.

'How is it that I know it when you lie?' he asked me sipping his cappuccino and smiling mischievously.

'You don't!' I said in mock anger and shock.

He smiled. In fact, both of us smiled a lot during the hour we got to spend with each other. I have no clue what is happening. Absolutely no clue!

12

The Damsel in Distress and the Knight in Shining Armour

28 June 2009

1.00 p.m.

Ananya has been acting very weird of late. She is perpetually glued to her phone something which has never happened before and thereby makes me extremely suspicious. I'm quite sure she is seeing someone, and is hiding the fact from me as well as Varun. Last night I saw her on the terrace, talking over the phone at around midnight. She did not come down for another full hour. I was still wide awake, busy sending deliciously clandestine messages to Rajeev sir when I saw her come down.

'Babes? Is that you?' I shouted from my room even though I knew for sure who it was. Ananya came into my room a minute later.

'Yeah, you are not asleep yet?' she asked intelligently.

'No, but neither are you,' I pointed out equally intelligently.

'What are you doing up so late?' she asked.

'Oh...well...generally you know...messaging.' I said casually. Of course, I could not tell her about Rajeev sir.

'Messaging who?' she asked.

'Mum,' I lied.

Anu nodded her head.

'You were on the phone?' I asked casually.

'Yes,' she said.

'With whom?' I asked.

'Mum,' pat came the reply.

Hmmm. Interesting, very interesting.

30 June 2009

2.00 p.m.

We are both in office and Ananya continues with her weird behaviour here as well. And I am fascinated now. Of course, not fascinated in the nosy Bubbly aunty way, just curious in an intelligent, MBA educated girl way.

However, I will concentrate on my life and not butt my nose in someone else's matters. That is the dignified twenty-first century woman way of doing things.

2.30 p.m.

I have just seen her pick up her phone and leave her seat. I think I will follow her out of the cubicle.

2.31 p.m.

I think if I hide behind the huge pillar, I will be able to listen to her, without her spotting me. But of course, I will not stoop to such level of scheming, rampant only in *Saas-Bahu* tv serials. It reminds one of the vampish *bahu* who wears a kaanjevaram silk sari with full makeup boiling milk in the kitchen at six o'clock in the morning. All her time in the kitchen is utilised in planning the murder of the quintessentially angelic albeit poor *choti bahu*.

But I digress.

2.32 p.m.

Of course, I will not hide behind the pillar. That's a sneaky way of finding out stuff which, in the very first place, I am not really even interested in.

2:32:01

I followed Ananya and am hiding behind the pillar from where I can hear her speak clearly.

'Sweetie...cummon,' she positively crooned.

Manly, boy-bashing, business like, sensible, wholly unromantic, I-cannot-stand-shopping-and-other-girlie-nonsense Ananya crooned into the handset. Literally crooned. If I were not so keen on knowing what happens next, I would have fainted there and then.

I-wear-only-men's-watch, I-hate-salwar-kurtas, I-don't-have-time-for-boys Ananya.

Karate classes Ananya. What is the world coming to? I felt trouble in my bronchial tubes. Breathing became difficult.

'Sugar lump,' said Ananya.

She waited for a few seconds listening intently. She then smiled.

'Marsh mellow.'

Silence. Giggle.

'Cup cake.'

Silence. Giggle.

'Chocolate fudge.'

This went on for some time. I started to loose interest in the list of desserts she was rattling off in a dreamy, sing-song voice. Both parties were either discussing food items for a party or were lovers appreciating each other by using worthy comparisons of their respective loved ones with food items. Judging by what I could see of her face and what I knew of her, I was quite sure it was the latter.

'Gotta go now!' hushed Ananya looking at her watch. That was my cue and I was already dashing out of sight when she turned around. And quite like a top notch investigative journalist, I was walking casually by Ananya's seat as she returned from her call, unmistakably a little red faced.

'All OK, babes?' I asked casually.

'Yeah.'

'On the phone?' I asked very airily pointing to her handset.

'Yeah,' she nodded.

'Mum?' I asked.

'Yeah, Mum,' she said trying to sound casual but avoiding my eyes.

Mum.

Yeah Right.

2 July 2009

Rather interestingly, I got a call from Purva today! I had the phone in my hands and I stared at it as it kept on ringing. I did not know whether I should even take his call after the conversation that has transpired between his mum and mine. Before I could make up my mind, the phone stopped ringing.

3 July 2009

Purva called again today. Unable to decide yet again whether I should pick up the phone or no, it stopped ringing by the time I decided to pick it up. But a few minutes later, I received a message from Purva.

'Hey...how are you doing? I don't mean to bug you but do give me a call if you get some time. Cheers.'

I felt a little weird and very curious once I read the message. What was it that the high and mighty Dr Purva, whose mother thinks I am too dark to be her daughter-in-law, want to talk to me about? With these noble thoughts in my mind, I dialled Purva's number rather hesitatingly. Purva's dialler-tone '*O meri hansini*' played for a long time. I am not a music freak, in fact, I rarely listen to music, but I was so carried away by the song that I was shocked when the music ended abruptly and a gruff voice said 'Hi'.

'Hi Purva, Kasturi here,' I said introducing myself a little awkwardly.

'Hey Hi.'

'Hi.'

Again the nested loop problem.

'I got your message. You wanted to speak to me?' I questioned, a little scared of what he would say next. What if he tells me that he wants to marry me? Ok that will not happen. What if he screams at me because of what my mum had said to his mum? Hmm...that might certainly happen. The possibilities, I realised were immense and varied.

'Yeah, I did. Good to speak?'

'Yes. Sure.'

'Ummm...,' he did not quite know how to say what he wanted to,'...I don't know if you know but our mothers had a rather interesting conversation.'

I grimaced, ready to bark something rude at him if *he* said anything rude about my mum.

'I just want to apologise on my mother's behalf. She is not generally rude but from what I can gather this seems to be her fault. I am sorry.'

I stood silent.

'Really?' I said stupidly.

'What do you mean really?' he sounded amused.

'Errr...I mean. Don't worry. I am cool,' I smiled into the phone.

'Can you please apologise to your mum as well please?' he asked.

'Yeah! Sure.' Two 'please's' in one sentence. Nice. I smiled to myself.

'Good then,' he said.

'Great.'

'Bye, and have a nice day,' he said and disconnected without saying anything else. He had just called to apologise on behalf of his mother. No motive other than to say sorry for personal remarks made by his mother. That is just very very sweet!

4 July 2009

Today is Saturday but I still went to office.

Blush

Apart from the obvious reason for going to work (read Rajeev sir), there was another urgent office matter that needed dealing with on a high priority basis. Varun and I need to have a very critical discussion. It has been pending for a long time now and after an urgent meeting during lunch we decided that things could not be delayed any further.

I sent an email to the HR administration requesting the board room for a meeting with my dear colleague Varun Agarwal. The mail went like this:

Dear Ami,

I need to request the board room for an important session with co-management trainee, Varun Agarwal from finance. He has, very kindly, agreed to take me through a session in finance which, as you undoubtedly know, is essential for a better understanding of marketing. I would like to book the board room for Monday, 11:00 a.m. Please let me know what else is needed from my end to facilitate this learning process for myself.

Regards,
Kasturi Shukla (Management trainee, marketing, Delhi unit).

I then sent an email to Varun, copying my manager, Rajeev sir.

Hi Varun,

Thank you for agreeing to take me through a finance session. The board room has been booked for Monday for 11.00 a.m. HR administration says that they have huge demand for the board room this Monday but thanks to a mail from Rajeev sir, the same has been arranged along with white board and LCD as was requested by you.
Thank you once again for your time.

Regards,
Kasturi Shukla

And thus having booked a board room on a Monday morning, when it would be in peak demand, Varun and I are ready to discuss and develop strategy we now need to adopt to tackle a growing problem – Ananya and her clandestine love life!

5 July 2009

11.15 p.m.

Late night exchange of texts with Rajeev sir.

'Hey girl...what's up?'

'Hello, I am doing good, what about you, sir?' I replied trying to sound as professional as I could under the trying circumstances. Images of Rajeev sir on his knees in front of me came out of nowhere.

'Missing someone from office.'

My heart skipped a beat. The Rajeev sir in my head now had a red rose in his hands and was looking at me with undisputed love in his eyes. I breathed deeply and replied.

'Really? Are you making some PPT?'

Innocent. And an obtuse reference to the only work I do in office.

'No,' was the one word reply.

'Then?'

'Thinking ☺.'

'Of...?'

'That someone from office, who by the way makes great PPTs.'

The Rajeev sir in my head was now somewhere exotic in Europe, surrounded by white pigeons with soft romantic music playing in the background. I should write something really flirty now, I told myself urgently. Quick, something smart and sassy, quick.

'Oh.' I wrote back after due deliberation of some ten minutes.

Why cannot I think of saying flirty stuff? Why god, why? Sheesh!

'Will see you in office tomorrow?'

'Yes, of course – I have a session with Varun from finance tomorrow,' I wrote quite aware of using office resources to discuss Ananya's love life.

'He has made a PPT for basic training in finance, right?'

'Yes yes but of course sitting with him and having him explain stuff would make things much simpler for me,' I wrote back hurriedly.

The phone rang almost as soon as I had sent the message.

'Hey,' Rajeev sir said in a deep, dreamy voice.

'Yes sir,' I said trying to sound professional as my heart beat as fast as the winning race horse.

'I think I will attend the finance session with you. The one that Varun is taking up for you...,' he added helpfully.

'What? No!' I gasped.

'Why?'

'How will it add any value to you? You know it all!' I stuttered unable to think of anything better.

'Not really. Actually I am always a little confused about these finance things...plus I will get some time with the girl from office I seem to be missing quite often these days,' he said in a voice that made my heart melt and cheeks turn hot.

'Errr...ummm...yeah...sure....,' was all that I managed to say as I yet again found myself helplessly gasping for support. On the other end of the call, Rajeev sir broke into a deep throaty laugh that made me think, once again, of butter and microwaves.

Sigh!

'Goodnight,' he said '...honey,' he added after a second's pause.

Honey? Did he say 'honey'? I mean did he really??

'Good night,' I managed somehow. I was not able to breathe as I put down the receiver.

Honey.

HONEY?

HONEY!!!!

OH MY BLOODY GAWDDD!!! HONEY!!

6 July 2009

I have been living in a sometimes foggy sometimes rosy world ever since Rajeev sir said the magic word. A million questions have been bugging me and pulling and tugging at my heart, mind and soul ever since. Would he call some random girl, 'honey'? Did it mean something? Did it mean *anything*? If yes, then what does this mean? Does he like me? Like me in a romantic way?

Average looking, nerdy me? And the super cool, sexy Rajeev sir?

I was in a different world as I walked into the board room. It was a busy Monday morning but there was nothing on my mind except 'honey'.

Honey...

I sauntered in and out of the board room. I was early and Varun, always prone to being late, was nowhere to be seen. I had varied feelings. Sometimes endless thoughts disturbed my otherwise jovial self, making me feel suffocated; another minute, I felt empty...listless, too overwhelmed for words. I was wandering aimlessly outside the board room, when I stopped in my tracks. My eyes met those of Rajiv sir. His brown eyes were searching for mine. Our eyes locked and I could feel a current pass through me. I quickly turned my eyes away from his.

'This way, sir,' I said stupidly pointing towards the board room.

'I know that, Kasturi,' he said quietly looking intently at me. His eyes stayed on mine for an extra second scrutinising my face.

When I entered the board room I realised that Varun was already seated. He had set up his laptop and as I walked in with Rajeev sir my eyes fell on the LCD screen and what it displayed.

I was paralysed for a few seconds before I was anywhere close to being able to react again. As realisation dawned on me, panic set in. I could see the possibility of this being my last day in office. I shuddered.

I soon woke to the fact that apart from my bit, a lot of staring was anyways going on.

Varun was staring at Rajeev sir with his mouth open.

Rajeev sir, stunned, was staring at the LCD which showed the first slide of the PPT. The heading on the slide displayed in bold red (font size 40):

'A(nanya's) Love story: Can she fool us?
A systematic, mathematical analysis of Ananya'a love life!'

Taking our discussion the other day a little further, Varun always fond of PPTs, had actually made a PPT on Ananya's queer behaviour. The main slide, visible to all right now, had two big red hearts. One had Anu's picture and the other had a question mark. There were two little figures clothed in black at the bottom of the screen holding big magnifying glasses and wearing pointy hats. 'Varun and Kasturi, the investigative management trainees,' a voice bubble in small font informed anyone who had any doubt about us being involved in such tomfoolery.

Hume tumse pyaar kitna… served as the background music. I later came to know that he had even done a scenario analysis on who could be Ananya's boyfriend. Scenario number five was the balding, fumbling LSD.

As I wondered how such a thing could have happened, the sad realisation of my foolishness hit me like a bolt of lightning. I had completely forgotten to tell Varun that Rajeev sir, too, was coming for the meeting and that we would have to discuss Ananya later sometime.

HELL.

Ok. It is not that bad. I tried to breathe easy. It's only Rajeev sir. After all he is the one who called me 'honey' last night. We are not in deep shit.

At that precise moment, when my heart beat slowed down to a normal rate, in walked the CMO looking a little worried.

'I am so sorry guys, I am a little late. I hope I have not missed too much,' he breezed in, settling down not looking at any of us. Rajeev sir was standing in front of him fortuitously blocking his view of the screen.

Not really, sir, we have just been gaping at each other.

'Thanks Rajeev, for asking me to come! You are right, finance never really makes sense to us marketing people,' said the CMO very enthusiastically to Rajeev sir.

Varun, standing next to the keyboard with the 'Esc' button right next to his right hand, stood rooted to the ground, not able to even bat an eye lid. I tried making eye contact with him and gestured asking him to shut the PPT but he seemed to see through me.

'...LSD is just outside, he is very keen to see what Varun has to say,' the CMO remarked casually, with eyes glued on his blackberry as he chatted with Rajeev sir and replied to emails simultaneously.

I sensed a slight change in Varun as he heard of the incumbent arrival of LSD, the chief operating officer of a company that had made the fatal mistake of hiring us idiots. So far Varun had a merely constipated look on his face but now he looked positively dead white.

His world was coming to an end.

I did not disagree. In fact I was pretty sure that mine was too.

My eyes found Rajeev's and I looked miserably at him, tears welling up in my eyes. Varun continued to be rooted to the ground, his eyes wide and scared. Rajeev sir looked at me and then shot a quick glance at Varun.

'Oh my god!' exclaimed Rajeev sir very loudly slapping his forehead the very next second.

CMO turned sharply to look at him.

'What's wrong?' he asked in a voice that quivered for no reason.

'Sir! That PPT!! I think we have put the wrong pricing!!' said Rajeev sir, his voice revealed a sense of urgency.

'Not the one for Airkel?' exclaimed the CMO in a high pitched voice.

'Very much sir!' Rajev sir exclaimed in the same precipitated tone.

'Oh NO!!' CMO exclaimed again.

'Oh Yes!' exclaimed Rajeev sir.

I giggled in my head.

'You said Lakhan sir is outside?' said Rajeev sir taking matters into his capable hands.

'Yes,' said the CMO, his voice shaking further.

'Great! Let's go get him ASAP!' Rajeev sir slapping the desk in front of him for effect.

'Sir!' continued Rajeev sir impatiently as CMO bent down to gather his things, 'Sir, we have no time! Kasturi get sir's stuff,' Rajeev sir barked orders.

I nodded my head like a dutiful employee who could do no wrong.

'Sorry guys...we will do this some other time. Really sorry – my fault!' said Rajeev sir, shutting off the power to the laptop before CMO could look at the screen. As the LCD shut down with a meek beep, I mentally whooped with joy.

'That's OK sir,' stammered Varun, too shaken to grasp what had just happened.

'Sorry Kasturi...we appreciate your enthusiasm and we are glad to have people like Varun and you on board,' said the CMO quite apologitically.

'I had been looking forward to the session,' he added.

'Me too sir,' Varun added, awakening from the dead. Realisation hit Varun that we had somehow managed to escape disaster and his face soon broke into a wide albeit shaky grin. As I watched the CMO leave the room, I could feel relief wash over me like a huge tidal wave. My career had just been given a second life. It was unbelievable how stupid I had been. I shook my head still not fully understanding all that had happened.

Following the CMO out of the board room, as Rajeev sir walked past me he, yet again, looked deep into my eyes.

And winked.

And muttered under his breath, 'You owe me one, girl!'

'Anything!' I whispered, meaning it.

My knight in shining armour. I sighed to myself as my heart beat like crazy.

13

I *Labh Loo*

6 July 2009

I do not think I will ever hear the last of what almost happened because of my carelessness yesterday.

7 July 2009

Do you think it is possible for me to kill Varun and get away with it?

8 July 2009

We were in office and I was pretending, as usual, to work when Ananya came to my desk looking all stiff and weird.

'Hi Kas,' she said not looking at me.

'Hey babes,' I said not looking at her. What was wrong with Anu?

'Ummm....you know...'

'Yes?' I said encouragingly.

'Well...will you meet me at the Select City Food Court this Saturday?'

'Meet you? Anu, we do live in the same house, remember?' I said surprised.

'Yeah...I know I want to speak to you and Varun about something,' she clarified.

'Varun and I both work in the same office as you, you know?' I ventured to point out the known yet again.

'Shut up, are you coming or no?' threatened Ananya in a style more familiar to me.

'OK, I will come,' I said timidly.

'OK. Good,' said Ananya looking all exasperated with me.

'Hey can you help me with Pivots for a sec?' I asked looking at the excel sheet open in front of me. Ananya's eyes lit up at the sound of the word as she quickly grabbed my laptop.

9 July 2009

Mum called today, her voice shaking with excitement. I knew what was coming.

'Beta,' she said.

'Amma,' I replied.

'Lehman!' she said.

'Brothers,' I added.

'Shut up,' she said.

'Maaaaa,' I wailed.

'Listen, there is this guy whose parents your daddy and I have been speaking to for some time now. They are really nice people. Not like that doctor's parents!' she said as if she had suddenly tasted something bad, 'boy works in Lehman Brothers!' she said grandly.

'So?' I was going to be difficult today. Was I expected to swoon over and die with happiness just because the boy worked in a particular company?

'So, you are meeting him tomorrow,' concluded my mother.

'No, I am not,' I said too experienced now to be taken aback by her ambush technique.

'Yes, you are. He is taking you to Taj and the tables have been booked,' she added.

'What? How do you know that?' I asked in spite of myself.

'His mother told me!' replied my mother airily.

'I don't have time,' I used tactic number two.

'I know you do. You were planning to go shopping with Varun and now you have cancelled it,' she said.

'No I have not!' I exclaimed triumphantly. I had completely forgotten about the shopping bit. God only knows what would have happened had I not turned up for the shopping trip. God bless Mother.

'You might not have but I have,' she said grandly. She had been waiting to make this statement. I could hear the victory in her voice.

'W-H-A-T!' I could hardly speak.

'Yes,' mom said primly, 'I spoke to Varun sometime back and cancelled your shopping trip.'

Oh my god. Thank god I do not have a brother. What kind of a mother-in-law would my mother make?

'How could you?' I asked belligerently. I could not get myself to use 'dare' in place of 'could' even in that moment of fury.

'Because you are my darling little princess and I know what works best for you!' she crooned.

I sighed to myself. I was unquestionably angry, but I also knew that there was no use in reacting to mum's antics. If I said something, she would start crying and it will end only with me apologising profusely for no fault of mine. No point fighting with her, really, no point.

'Yes, I am your darling little princess,' I said half-heartedly. My voice was quiet but I was still very angry.

9 July 2009

10.00 p.m.

I got another text from Rajeev sir.

'Coffee misses you.'

I smiled. Sometimes he could be really cheesy.

'I don't miss coffee at all,' I replied playing along.

'Will you meet coffee for coffee tomorrow?'

'Why should I meet coffee when I do not like coffee?'

'Coffee is very hurt ☹. Coffee wants you to meet coffee because coffee has something very important to tell his sugar lump.'

My heart skipped a beat. What could Rajeev sir have to tell me? What?

10.02 p.m.

You know what? I think I know what Rajeev sir wants to tell me. If I have read those beautiful brown eyes correctly then my heart already knows what he wants to tell me. I know this seems like a dialogue from a Bollywood movie that might never be released but it is true.

10.03 p.m.

God, please please please let it be what I think it might be. Please.

10.04 p.m.

Oh and by the way, did I say 'please'?

11 July 2009

Rajeev sir and I met at Barista at seven in the evening. He was there by the time I reached and was sitting in a quiet corner reading a newspaper. He was wearing a red and blue check shirt and dark blue denims. His eyes smiled as they found mine.

I had taken a lot of care while dressing today. I had chosen a black skirt and a bright pink top to go with it.

We sat down and Rajeev sir ordered coffee for both of us. He was unusually quiet.

'Why are you so quiet today?' I asked him a little worried.

'Because I have something important to tell you and I do not know how you will react to it,' he said.

As he pulled his chair a little closer to mine, I felt weak in my knees.

'You smell lovely,' he said.

I gulped feeling a lump in my throat.

The waiter got us our coffee. Rajeev sir stirred his thoughtfully. There was some music playing in the background and I started humming to it.

'Okay,' said Rajeev sir after a few minutes as if he had finally made up his mind.

'Yes?' I asked casually but my heart was racing like a bull attacking the red cloth.

'See Kasturi the thing is...I really like you,' he said.

I fumbled for words. And why the hell was I behaving like a *gaon ki sharmeeli gori*.

'That's nice, you should like me. We work together – it would be horrible to work with someone you do not like,' I said. No, do NOT ask me why I said something as stupid as this. Please do not. This will go down as one of the biggest mysteries of all times.

'Kasturi!' Rajeev sir exclaimed. I smiled weakly, scared of what was coming next.

'See Kasturi, I need to tell you how I feel about you. Of course, I like you as a co-worker. As a friend, I more than like you.'

I looked at him as he seemed at a momentary loss of words.

'I think I am falling desperately and madly in love with you, Kasturi Shukla, and I see nothing that will stop me.' He declared as my heart did finally stop for a couple of seconds. Was this really happening or was this another of those dreams I had been having so often these days where Rajeev sir professes his undying love for me?

'Pinch me,' I ordered.

'I would much rather kiss you,' he said smiling.

Oh my god. I can say nothing right today. I had better shut up, I told myself. His hands found mine and his fingers wrapped around my wrist. His hands slid further along my arms till his fingers were entwined in mine. I looked at him. He smiled. I could see his dimples. I smiled.

'Do you not have anything to say, Kasturi?' he asked.

'No,' I said unthinkably.

'Do you like me?' he asked.

I nodded a yes.

'Do you love me?' he asked.

I blushed and nodded a yes.

'I love you,' Rajeev sir said.

On the sofa next to us, a young mother was sitting with her two-year-old toddler. As the little boy heard Rajeev say the words, he shook his mop of curly hair, raised his round, big, black, innocent eyes towards his mother and said, 'I labh loo' as his mother broke into peals of laughter.

I will not forget that moment for as long as I live.

12 July 2009

Okay, so let's get this straight for the sake of posterity. On 11 July 2009, the proverbial man of my dreams confessed his undying love for me. I literally died of happiness. But what am I doing today?

I am sitting in front of Lehman!

Yes, Lehman and I met at Taj. The meeting had been set and no arguments from my side would cancel/postpone it. Of course I could not give my mum the real reason. She might die of shock and I did not want her blood on my hands.

The highlight of our meeting was undoubtedly the conversation. It was almost beyond interesting and I listened to him in rapt attention. Lehman spoke for some half an hour about the 300cr business his father owns, the next half an hour was dedicated to the eleven houses they own, the next half was reserved solely for the petrol pump off the Ludhiana highway which is bringing in bucket loads of money. The next quarter was dedicated to how in spite of being born with a silver spoon in his mouth, Lehman always valued studies. The next was for how he never really had to slog, it just came so naturally to him. The remaining 200 hours were dedicated to Lehman Brothers and how only the best make it inside the hallowed portals of the company.

I think I tried to speak for about half a micro second and then gave up. He seemed keen to speak his heart out to me so like a patient, tolerant mother I let Lehman bray.

I tried to concentrate on the walls of the restaurant. For the simple reason that they were infinitely more interesting. The giant clock seemed broken. I looked at the watch. 7. 40. I looked at it again after what seemed like three to four hours of Lehman's nonstop I-me-myself and it still showed 7:41:23.

I hardly ordered anything for myself, not that Lehman noticed or bothered. He was too busy talking about this other six storied house his Dad was thinking of buying. And hence it was no surprise that as soon as Lehman sipped the last sip of his lemonade I got up.

'Time to go!' I chirped happily.

'Uh...I have hardly told you anything about myself!' wailed Lehman looking quite stricken. His lips curled downwards in a hilarious inverted 'U'.

'Ohh...right, the last few hours were all about your cars and *your* house and *your* company,' I agreed.

'Yes,' he agreed solemnly nodding his head like a school boy in front of his teacher. I have often noticed that such sarcasm goes unnoticed by self-obsessed people.

'See you later then,' I said airily and walked off.

11 July 2009

Rajeev sir and I went for coffee again. I love every second I get to spend with him.

12 July 2009

No. of hours spent with Rajeev sir: 1.5

No of hours spent thinking about the 1.5 hours spent with Rajeev Sir: fifteen

13 July 2009

11.30 p.m.

So, I got ready to meet Ananya all the while wondering why she had arranged for such a meeting. She, herself, had mysteriously disappeared at about noon making it look all the more suspicious. As I was leaving my house I got a text from Rajeev sir.

'What's up, honey?' he asked.

Honey almost died as she does each time she is called honey. I hastily replied to his text which then led to a flurry of texts which made a blush tomato red at such a frequency that it was quite alarming. So some one hour later I was in a rickety rick still replying to texts from Rajeev sir which would put anyone to shame. I had half an eye on the auto rickshaw *waley bhaiya*, who was doing very un-*bhaiya* like things by turning his head around to leer at me at every alternate second.

Once we reached the destination, I was only too glad to see the last of him and I paid him the fifty bucks without haggling even a little bit (which is basically against my rules and ethics). His hand brushed purposefully against mine as he took the money. I turned away in disgust. I love Delhi to bits, but there are certain things about the city that I abhor.

I sighed and turned away to face the street. I squinted my eyes as I recognised Ananya's electric blue shirt from across the road. I wondered, yet again, why she had gotten me here. What did she wish to talk about?

I soon saw Ananya look at me from across the street. I waved at her. She waved back as she started to cross the road. She started to mouth something at me from mid-way across the street. I could not understand what she was saying. I shrugged my shoulders. What could not wait another few seconds? After a moment's pause Ananya started gesticulating again. I was however not looking at her. My gaze was frozen in the other direction – opposite to the direction of the incoming traffic – at the one lone auto that was crazily careening its way, avoiding traffic as it moved at a high speed in the wrong lane. It was the same auto that had gotten me here. But that was not what had attracted my attention. What had grabbed my attention was the simple fact that the auto seemed to be heading straight into Ananya who, busy gesticulating at me, was blissfully unaware.

The second the realisation hit me I started screaming madly at Ananya. But before I knew it, in front of my very eyes, I saw the auto hit Ananya as if in slow motion. The auto hit Ananya with such force that she was thrown a few feet in the air. Tires screeched.

I screamed.

14

The Dark Hour

I screamed.

A lady next to me dropped the bags she was carrying. The moment stood still as I felt blood drain out of my face.

I sprinted madly towards Ananya's body that seemed to be too still on the road, a few feet away from me. A small crowd had gathered around Ananya in the few seconds it took me to reach her side. No one had touched her. Her leg was twisted at an odd angle and she was face down.

Once next to her, I did not really know what to do. After a few seconds, I knelt down and with shivering hands turned her face to face mine. My heart sank and I started perspiring profusely as I saw her face all red with blood.

I felt I could not breathe.

'Please help!!!' I begged the crowd around me. Someone handed me a bottle of water. A man knelt down near Ananya and touched her wrist.

'There is no pulse,' he said.

My mouth went dry. I could not breathe. My hands started shaking uncontrollably.

Ananya. Dead?

The crowd gasped collectively. Another man stepped forward. 'There is too much blood everywhere,' he said.

I felt faint. What was happening? Surely this was just a bad dream. I will wake up and will hear the horrible music Ananya likes to play early in the morning.

'Please call a doctor. Please someone,' I screamed as I found my voice.

Ananya's hair was drenched with blood; her hands were limp – there seemed to be no life. I absently noted that the crowd had doubled in size in the last few minutes and everyone seemed to be saying something. I was not able to hear anything no matter how much I tried. Why was I acting like such a wussy? I chided myself the next second surprised at my weak behaviour.

Hold yourself together, Kasturi. What you do can probably make a big difference now. Each second mattered. I picked up Ananya's hand and felt her pulse. No, there was no pulse. Ok. Maybe a weak one. I felt a glimmer of hope. I put my hand on her throat under her ears. I could feel something throb.

There is life in her. She is not dead. Not dead.

I told myself fiercely. Not dead! I pulled out my mobile with great purpose. I knew who I was going to call as I confidently dialled the numbers. The phone kept ringing and dad did not respond. Panic again started settling in. I suddenly realised that there was another person I could call. I did not hesitate even for a second as I dialled the unfamiliar number.

'Dr Purva speaking,' said the oddly familiar voice on the other end.

15

Revelations

'Hello...hello...is anyone there?' said Purva as I took a second to find my voice. I was already feeling a lot calmer just listening to his quiet voice.

'Purva! This is Kasturi. I need your help. My friend has been hit by an auto and is lying in a pool of blood in the middle of the road and I have no idea what to do!' I said oddly calm and hysterical at the same time.

'Ok. Don't panic. Breathe. Check her pulse,' came the calm response.

'Weak,' I said.

'Not bad, bleeding?'

'Heavy!'

'From?'

'I do not know...everywhere it seems.'

'OK. Don't panic. Lay her flat on the road; do NOT put her head in your lap.'

'OK Purva.'

'You know the nearest hospital?'

'No,' I said.

'Where are you?'

'Outside Select City Mall.'

'Stay put, an ambulance is on its way,' and with that the line went dead. I stared at the phone in my hand. I was fine till Purva was on the line. The moment he disconnected the call, I started panicking.

'Take her to the hospital,' someone from the crowd shouted at me.

'No get a doctor here!' another man shouted. I looked bewildered at the unfamiliar faces shouting instructions at me. I knew I was wasting precious time. I panicked further. The phone in my hands started ringing. Purva's name flashed on the screen.

'Ok, how are we now?' asked Purva taking command of the situation.

'Purva, please stay on the line with me,' I pleaded with him.

'Yes, Kasturi. I will. I was just giving orders for the ambulance. I am right here,' said Purva.

'Ok. These people here are asking me to take her to some other hospital close by.'

'Ok. Ask the name of the hospital.'

I gave him the name.

'No, don't do that. AIMMS ambulance should be there in another ten seconds.'

Almost as soon as he finished the sentence, I could hear the siren of the approaching ambulance. The next couple of hours are a confused, hazy, scared blur now. Ananya was rushed into emergency where a bed was ready for her when we reached. Purva was there, in his white coat looking so different from the only time I had seen him that I almost did not recognise him. As soon as we came in, Purva and his team took complete charge.

I could hear Purva give orders as his hands moved gently and firmly with a million tubes, syringes and machines.

By this time I had gotten some twenty calls from Varun who was still at Select City waiting for us. As I got a breather I called him and gave him the horrific news. Within minutes, Varun was by my side. It was only once Varun came that I broke down into uncontrollable tears. Varun patted me uncomfortably before pulling me in big bear hug as I cried harder. We spent the next few minutes in the hospital temple and prayed for our friend.

As we made our way back to Ananya's room, I saw Purva come out looking very tense.

'Purva! How is Anu?' I asked fearing the worst.

'She is OK,' said Purva, smiling, 'or rather, she is going to be fine. She has had a concussion from the fall, one broken hand, two broken ribs and one broken leg. The good news is that none of this is life threatening and a full recovery is expected, though the recovery itself will take time and can be quite painful,' rattled off Purva addressing both Varun and me.

Varun and I waited outside Anu's room for what remained of the day, anxious and scared, with no one for comfort other than each other. Varun and I. We were in this together. I knew this and drew a lot of comfort from the thought in the lone, dark hours that followed Anu's accident.

Much later in the night as the ward grew quieter, I quietly stepped inside Ananya's room and stood next to her bed for an eternity. Ananya was too sedated to know that I was around. She had not and was not expected to regain consciousness. In the darkness as I looked at her frame wrapped in gauge and stared at the many machines attached to her body which seemed oddly tiny now, I felt tears well up in my eyes. It was, after all, in a way my fault. Had she not been trying to talk to me while crossing the road this might have never happened. I thought about how painful the recovery will be. Dr Purva had already warned us about it. The accident seemed so surreal, as if it was always meant to happen. I relived the accident again and again. I felt goose bumps on my hand as I thought about that one moment, when I took Ananya to be dead. I shuddered each time I thought about it. How different my life had been before the accident. I never really realised how close Anu and I had become of late. It was only now that it dawned upon me. Her pain seemed to be mine; her discomfort seemed to belong to me. I wanted to do every possible thing on this planet that would make it all OK for her. It was weird, as I have never had a friend for whom I have felt this way. I thought about Anu's idiotic manners, her stupid way of cooking and her untidy way of living. It made me smile through my tears.

I do not know for how long I had been standing there thinking these random thoughts about Ananya, silent tears streaming down my face when I heard a faint, polite cough.

Purva was standing next to me. He looked tired but had a kind smile on his face that warmed my heart. Purva. He had been such a thorough gentleman all through, right from the time we exchanged our first email.

'Hey,' he said softly.

I smiled weakly through my tears.

'Come on!' he said gently as he pulled me away from Ananya's bed.

'Have you eaten anything?' he asked as we walked in the corridor.

That made me cry harder because that was exactly the kind of question my dad would have asked.

'No,' I said in between tears.

'I guessed as much,' he said handing me a tissue to wipe my tears and asked me to follow him. We walked quietly through the corridors. All was silent yet the corridors brimmed with activity. Purva said a word or two to the occasional nurses/doctors that walked past us. In about five minutes we reached the canteen. Purva took me to a quiet corner and sat me down.

'What do you want to eat?' he asked looking at my tear strained face with concern.

'I am not hungry,' I said wiping my tears.

'Ok,' he said slowly.

'Purva...,' I started but stopped midway suddenly unsure about what I really wanted to say. I felt at a loss of words.

'Yes?' he looked up from under his eye brows and scar.

'Thank you,' I said as my voice cracked again and fresh tears welled up in my eyes.

'Oh god... Kasturi please... I am a doctor, it's my job.'

'I don't care if it was your job or not. All I know is that I had no one to turn to when you helped me out. I... have... no... no idea what I would have done had you not been around. I... I...' I said in between tears unable to continue.

'Relax please, Kasturi. And if it helps, you are welcome,' he smiled as he put a comforting hand on my arm. There was just something so nice about his kind, calm voice and gentle smile that I felt I could trust him with anything, not just my friend's life.

'We got Ananya in time, she is going to be fine. There is really no need to worry,' he said as he hungrily scanned the menu.

'You seem hungry,' I observed changing the topic.

'It's almost three in the morning and the last bit of food I had was at seven yesterday morning,' he said grimly. I smiled a weak smile.

He ordered one *aloo parantha* for himself. As I made small talk with Purva, my cell beeped. It was a message from Rajeev sir. I had called him at the first opportunity I had found after getting Ananya to the hospital. Although he did pick up the phone, all I could hear was really loud music. It seemed that he was in a disc and was quite unable to hear what I was saying. Also, he seemed to be blabbering nonsense and with a million doctors hovering over Anu, I had no patience to deal with it then. I had simply cancelled the call. But as an afterthought I had messaged him about Ananya's accident. Even though I did not receive a reply, I kept messaging him updates more for the need of fooling myself into believing that I had some support than anything else. I felt angry with him now that I saw his name on the screen of my phone.

'Sad to hear about Ananya. I hope she is OK now,' – was all that the text read. I deleted the text as I felt anger surge inside me. Rajeev sir will have to wait. By this time Purva's *aloo parantha* had arrived and Purva had started digging hungrily into it.

Purva saw me staring at his plate, he said, 'OK I can give you one small bite. Nothing more.'

The *parantha* looked absolutely delicious, smelled heavenly and more importantly my stomach growled a huge approval.

'OK, just a very tiny piece,' I said as if doing him a favour. Purva pushed his plate towards me so that it stood mid way between us. I broke a little piece of the *parantha* and was toying with it when Purva pushed the bowl of curd towards me. I dipped the *parantha* into the curd and quickly put it in my mouth. I kept staring at his plate as he ate without seeming to bother with me. I quietly slid my hand to the plate and broke off another piece off Purva's *parantha*. Purva did not seem to notice and continued to eat in silence. He finally looked at me when I broke off the fourth piece.

'I will order another one?' he asked grinning.

I nodded. 'Order at least three,' I said smiling for the first time in the day.

Purva's eyes crinkled around their edges as he smiled a wide victorious smile!

'Sure,' he said as he called out to the waiter.

So there I was, at three o'clock in the morning, in the AIMMS canteen, with a friend in the emergency ward, sitting in front of Purva, eating *aloo paranathas* from his plate and feeling better than I had felt in the last ten hours.

There are many things that make two people bond in a very special way. And, as I have realised today, sharing *aloo paranthas* at three in the morning from the same plate is definitely one of them. As I looked at Purva concentrating on his food with single minded focus there was just one thought in my head.

Thank you, god, for Purva. I don't think I will ever be able to repay him for what he has done for me today. He was there when I had no one to turn to. Thank you for him. Thank you.

14 July 2009

9.00 a.m.

Varun called up Ananya's mother to inform her of the accident. Apparently he got quite a screechy earful for not having informed or called her earlier. Anu's mom is on her way to Delhi and should be here latest by tomorrow. Wow, so apart from a friend with all limbs broken, I will now have to deal with a screeching mother? Life really cannot get any better, can it?

Also, Rajeev sir has not bothered to call yet. Why is he never there when I need him?

12.00 noon.

Received a text from Rajeev sir.

'How is my sweetheart doing?'

'In the hospital.'

'WHAT! ARE YOU ALL RIGHT?'

I felt a little perplexed and I messaged him once more about Ananya.

Turns out that he was out with his friends late afternoon onwards and had not even bothered to read the text properly. Hence the curt reply yesterday. He has promised to come to the hospital immediately. Though his explanation does not really make much sense to me and I can ask a dozen questions, I just do not want to get into that right now.

12.30 p.m.

Rajeev came with a HUGE bouquet of flowers for Ananya, lots of fruits and some chocolates. He dropped all the bags he was carrying as soon as he saw me and opened his arm wide. I looked at his open arms with a questioning look on my face.

'Come here!' he ordered smiling. My anger evaporated as I took unsure and shy steps to cross the length of the hospital room towards him.

'Honey, are *you* OK?' he said, concern written all over his gorgeous face as he pulled me into an embrace. Our first hug. I had spent numerous office hours wondering how it would make me feel if it does happen. In turns, I had imagined the Swiss Alps and the Egyptian pyramids in the background of our first hug, a far cry from the impersonal, white hospital room. As Rajeev sir hugged me tighter, I realised that I was physically closer to Rajeev sir than I had ever believed I could be. I did not know what to do or how to behave or what to say or how to breathe. I also seemed to have too many hands and feet and did not quite know what to do with them.

Breathe Kasturi, breathe, I reminded myself.

Breathe in, I did. And as I did that, I inhaled his perfume that made my head swim. The top of my head barely reached his chin. Both his arms were around my waist, holding me tight as he buried his face in my hair. I tried desperately to memorise all that I could about that moment. In spite of the very unromantic setting it was just perfect. I was in the perfect, strong, lean arms of the perfect guy. It could not get better than this.

He pulled away all too soon.

'How is she?' he asked pointing towards Ananya.

'I am very angry!' I exclaimed setting my face in what I thought was delicate moue as I ignored his question.

'I am really sorry, Kasturi, really really sorry,' said Rajeev sir not yet letting go of my hand.

'Where were you the whole of last night?' I asked in spite of myself.

'I am sorry, please do not be angry!' he pleaded.

I was about to question Rajeev sir further when I heard Ananya moan. Rajeev sir and I turned around to look back at Ananya. She was stirring for the first time since the accident. I rushed to her side and put my hand gingerly on the side of her face that was not scarred. Her mouth seemed too dry.

'Anu? Are you okay?' I asked worried and relieved at the same time.

Ananya moaned in response.

Telling Rajeev sir that I will be back in a second and asking him to keep an eye on Anu, I rushed out to hunt for a familiar nurse or doctor. Luckily enough I found Purva coming out of one of the hospital wards.

'Ananya's regained consciousness,' I said catching my breath.

'Great,' he said as we walked quickly towards Ananya's room.

Purva was at Anu's bed side the instant we reached Ananya room. He checked Ananya, asking her questions in a voice that seemed confident and concerned at the same time, gingerly touching her while taking care to not cause more pain than was necessary. I could not help but notice how his movements and mannerisms were both firm and gentle. Although Ananya seemed to be dazed with the great pain she responded to Purva's gentle words.

'You are going to be fine,' he smiled at Ananya finishing the check-up. I might be wrong but I could see an expression of great relief on Purva's face. The examination had showed results he had been hoping for but was not really expecting, 'There shall be no permanent damage, Ananya, you will be absolutely fine,' added Purva.

'You are in good hands,' Purva said, 'and you have excellent friends,' added Purva waving a careless hand in my direction much to my embarrassment.

Ananya's tired and heavy eyes looked around the room and rested on my face. Half raising her hand in acknowledgement, she tried to smile but it ended up just being a grimace as another bout of pain hit her. I could read her eyes, looking at me with gratitude and love. They thanked me. A heartfelt thank you that

I was only too happy to accept. I nodded my head and smiled at her. She closed her eyes soon after leaving me to my thoughts.

Having made a few notes on Ananya's medical chart, Purva was about to leave the room when his eyes fell on Rajeev sir. He looked questioningly at me.

'Rajeev, this is Purva, Ananya's doctor,' I said introducing Purva to Rajeev as the two men stood face to face.

'And Purva, this is Rajeev...my...err...mm...our...' I faltered, unsure. Rajeev, my boss? Rajeev, our colleague from work? Rajeev my friend?

Rajeev sir looked at me from under his eyes, smiling to himself aware of the dilemma I was facing. He took a few steps that brought him very close to me. He stood there smiling mischievously at me for a few minutes.

'*Hum Aapke Hain Kaun?*' he said in his suave sexy voice.

'That is very VERY corny!' I said blushing, as usual, in spite of myself as our eyes locked

Someone coughed. That woke me up. I blushed again as I saw Purva looking at me with confused eyes. For a second I had completely forgotten that he was in the room.

'Hi doc, I am Rajeev, Kasturi's boyfriend,' said Rajeev sir with unmistakable pride in his voice. I was stunned. Boyfriend? Kasturi's boyfriend. First, it was difficult to digest the fact that geeky, nerdy Kasturi had a boyfriend. And add to the fact that the boyfriend was none other than the super sexy Rajeev sir and you have breaking news! While I could see no expression on Purva's face, I felt inexplicably embarrassed in front of him for a reason I could not quite identify.

'Nice to meet you, Rajeev,' said Purva, 'you are one lucky man,' was all that Purva said as he walked quickly past us.

14 July 2009

I was feeding Ananya some absolutely disgusting hospital soup when I heard a woman's voice screaming down the usually quiet corridor.

'I am looking fatter,' the shrill voice seemed to resonate through the corridors. I giggled but stopped myself as I saw Ananya's face which had turned a weird shade of white 'These uncivilised people,' I said primly feeling quite superior, 'they have no prevailing civic sense and are steadily going down the ladder of civility,' I whispered to her thinking that she was getting irritated with all the noise. Ananya had recently shown a lot of improvement but was still under observation and had a long way to go before she could leave the hospital. I had been trying my best to make everything as comfortable for her as was possible.

She grimaced further as the wailing from the woman increased in volume.

'Where the hell is my daughter?' the uncouth, uncivilised but now clearer voice shrilled down our corridor. I giggled mentally as I thought what I had heard a little while ago and for the first time felt glad about who my mother was.

Seeing the pained look on Ananya's face, I set down the soup bowl with purpose and as I walked past the door of our room I bumped head on into something huge from which was emanating the same shrill voice, only now I knew who it was directed at.

Ananya.

'Beta,' in a dramatic filmy rush, the fat aunty ran at amazing speed to the bed side of her now visibly disturbed daughter. She was wearing a crisp cotton sari and had put on heavy makeup. She looked exceptionally authoritative and ill-tempered. I took an instant dislike to her.

'Ma!' croaked Ananya sadly, looking quite forlorn.

'Betaaaaa,' wailed the fat aunty.

'Why are *you* here?' asked Ananya, looking hostile even when wrapped in bandages.

'Look at you! Who did this? Tell me who did this to you? I will not leave him!' fat aunty said angrily. It sounded more like Ananya had been raped than hit by a speeding auto.

Ananya rolled her eyes.

'You!' fat aunty pointed at me, 'who are you?'

I felt scared.

'I am Kasturi, Ananya's friend from office,' I said timidly.

'Do you know who I am?' she demanded. Ananya grimaced.

'Ananya's mom?' I answered helpfully.

'I am the DM of Arbipur, I am an IAS officer!' she said disregarding my helpful input.

'Wow,' I thought that if there was going to be any time in my life to show my admiration and respect for the Indian Administrative Services, now was it.

'Who did this to my daughter?' she demanded of me again.

'An auto driver,' I said.

'Which auto driver?' she asked angrily impatient at how slow I was.

'I don't know his name,' I said lamely.

'Oh don't be so stupid!' she said angrily, 'were you there when the accident happened? Did you see that man's face?'

My auto driver, the dark man, with a moustache and weird eyes flashed in my head.

'Yes, I think I did,' I said slowly as the realisation and hence its significance hit home. I was the only person who had seen the auto driver.

'You did, Kas?' asked Ananya looking at me surprised.

'You did?' finally some words came out of Varun's mouth as he stood there staring at fat aunty.

'Yes I did,' I said looking down feeling guilty for having seen his face.

'Why did you not tell me before?' demanded fat aunty in a shrill voice.

One, because I had no clue that the 500kgs that comprises of you existed and two, because I was so busy trying to save the life of your precious little Beta that I did not even think about eating and drinking, leave alone anything else.

'Dubey! Come here,' Ananya's mother barked the order to the so far invisible Dubey ji.

A meek looking Dubey ji in a khaki suit materialised from behind the door in no time.

'Take her to the police station and find the man who did this to my daughter!' she said angrily, 'I will end his life and his career,' she finished breathlessly.

'I don't want to go to the police station,' I said defiantly, very scared at the thought.

'Mom, Kas is not going to the police station!' Ananya said as angrily as she could but her voice still sounded little more than a croak.

'I don't want to go,' I reiterated my point getting more and more scared. Visions of a dank, dark police station with a fat police inspector leering at me from behind his moth-eaten desk came to my mind with surprising frequency in the next couple of minutes.

'Ananya, you are not well. Shut up,' shrilled the fat aunty.

'No ma'am, Ananya is not going there all alone!' said Varun sounding very unsure even to me.

Fat IAS aunty did not bother to glare at Varun for more than two seconds. He was a dead fly in a glass of milk and she did not wish to waste her precious time on dead flies.

'Dubey! Take this girl to the police station and get her to sketch the man.' She sounded like the red queen from *Alice in Wonderland*. Off with her head.

'I do not wish to go,' I said getting as angry as I was now scared.

'Kasturi is not going anywhere she does not wish to go ma'am,' a now familiar feeling of relief washed over me as the gentle yet firm voice of Purva fell on my ears. All faces including that of fat aunty turned towards Purva as he walked in looking all dapper in his white doctor's coat, stethoscope around his neck and a file in his hand.

'Hello, I am Dr Purva Dikshit. The patient there,' he said pointing to Ananya, 'is under my care and the lady there,' he said pointing to me, 'is a close friend. She does not wish to go to the police station alone with Dube ji, who with all due respect to him, is an unknown man for Kasturi. Do you think ma'am, we can get the sketch artist here? Ananya needs Kasturi around anyways as Kasturi has been taking care of Ananya and knows her medicines better than anyone,' he said reasonably, in a calm controlled voice.

I have noticed that Purva's voice has a weird effect on people. It calms them and soothes their nerves. Fat IAS aunty seemed ready to retort but then thought the better of it. A second latter she seemed to relax visibly.

'Yes, we can do that,' she finally relented.

The tension in the air decreased.

'Can I have a word with you doctor?' she asked in a shrill voice and led Purva out of the door. This was the first time I had seen Purva since he had met Rajeev. And I don't know why but I got this distinct feeling that Purva was not too happy about Rajeev sir though he had been perfectly nice about the whole thing. Too nice, maybe.

I was lost in my thoughts when I heard a sniff. I turned around to see poor Ananya in tears. Alarmed, I rushed to her side.

'Ananya! Are you in pain? Are you OK?' I asked horrified to see her in tears.

'That's my mom...she did not even ask me if I was ok,' she said with tears streaming down her face.

'That's OK...she is concerned about you...and is trying to find the auto guy,' I tried to reason things out. I, too, had noticed how totally devoid of any tenderness aunty's behaviour had been.

Ananya's frail body shook with quiet sobs as I stood next to her bed with my hand on her shoulder, wiping her tears with a piece of gauze. Varun came and stood close by and put a hand on Anu's other shoulder. We stood there, for a long time, lost in our thoughts. It was all quiet for a long, long time but for Ananya's quiet sobs.

15 July 2009

Today is my first day in office after Ananya's accident. I don't know how to behave with Rajeev sir now. No clue. I cannot believe that I am now supposedly seeing someone. Last night Rajeev sir changed his relationship status on Facebook from 'single' to 'in a relationship'. Last I checked, thirty-four people had liked the update and twenty-three people had commented. Rajeev sir had refused to divulge the name of the girl on Facebook.

My knight in shining armour!

11.00 a.m.

Why does my heart stop beating when I catch a glimpse of Rajeev sir? Why? Why? Why?

2.00 p.m.

I have not gotten any work done, even though I have three PPTs to make and two more to beautify. With so much work, most of which I could outsource to ten-year-old Kasturi, I should not waste time staring at the door of Rajeev sir's cabin.

4.00 p.m.

I was standing next to the water cooler in a quiet corner in the office staring at my phone just to check once again if there was any message from Rajeev sir when suddenly someone grabbed my waist from behind. I was about to scream involuntarily when a large hand clamped on my mouth and I found myself staring into the dark brown eyes of Rajeev sir.

'Hey,' he said.

'Let go!' I said as he removed his hand from my mouth. I giggled in spite of myself. Gosh! How does he tolerate the perpetually giggly me!

'No, I won't.'

'Please.'

'On one condition.'

'Which is?'

'Say that you love me?'

I smiled shyly.

'It kills me, you know,' he said as I looked quizzically at him, 'when you smile like that.'

My smile widened into a grin.

'It kills me, you know,' he said as I continued to grin, 'when you grin like that.'

I buried my face into his shoulder, electricity running through me.

'Say that you love me,' he insisted.

'I love you.'

'I love *you,*' he said as he pulled me closer.

Someone coughed in the corridor nearby. We hurriedly and very reluctantly pulled apart as we heard footsteps approaching. By the time the LSD, to whom the footsteps belonged, reached us, we were standing apart with a very respectable distance between us. A man with a keener eye for subtleties than LSD might have noticed my tomato red cheeks and made an accurate guess about what Rajeev sir and I had been up to. But no, not LSD. Unless things are mentioned as numbers in excel sheets or bullet points in PPTs, he does not really get it. Thank god for that!

'So what have the two of you been up to?' asked the CEO quite innocently. He did not know what the honest answer would do to his weak heart.

'Sir, we have been having a heated discussion about the future of the telecom sector. Kasturi has just made an exceptionally intelligent observation that has quite stumped me,' Rajeev sir said seriously.

'Really, Kasturi, why don't you share it with us again? I would love to know what you have observed,' LSD said encouragingly. His broad smile displayed his now famous teeth.

I groaned mentally and glared at Rajeev sir as I thought ferociously about something intelligent to say.

16 July 2009

'I am seeing Rajeev sir,' I announced. The very next instant four eyes as big as saucers were staring at me in disbelief.

It was around eight in the evening and both Varun and I had come to the hospital straight from work. We had just finished a quiet and rather disgusting hospital food dinner with Ananya. Varun was reading a book and Ananya was resting with her eyes closed. I had been pondering about how someone, no anyone, could possibly make such bad soup when suddenly without a warning this came out of me. My dad has always been right. Very good food and very bad food – both weaken the man.

'What?' Varun shrieked in a high pitched voice. I observed that Varun did not close his mouth after he finished saying his 'what'.

'By Rajeev sir do you mean Rajeev Mehrotra from office?' croaked Ananya as she sat up in shock. Dr Purva had been asking Ananya repeatedly to start sitting up for the last two days. It finally took five words from me to do the trick.

I nodded my head looking at the shocked faces with increasing amusement.

'Like *seeing him* seeing him? I mean like romantically?' croaked Ananya. This was the maximum she had spoken in one go since the accident without stammering or pausing for breath. The wonders of true love, I mused philosophically to myself picturing loads of happy little cupids and little red hearts floating in the air.

'Yes,' I said dreamily.

'When did this happen?' she asked.

'A couple of weeks back,' I said.

'He is from IPPM!' said Varun accusingly. He had shut his mouth and opened it again when he felt strong enough. He distinctly resembled a fish I had as a pet when I was little. I had named him Mr Mouth.

'So?'I said defensively.

'Is not that hilarious!' he said, 'are you daring to dream beyond the IIMs?' he added trying to not laugh.

Ananya, too, started smiling broadly.

'Shut up!' I said irritated and turned my face away from him.

From behind my back I heard Varun burst into fits of uncontrolled laughter the next instant. I turned to look at Ananya for support only to find her shaking with silent laughter. Slowly, I felt my frown being replaced by a smile and sooner than I had expected I too was howling with laughter for no apparent reason.

And with that for the first time in what seemed like ages, the three of us were laughing again. It was then, at that precise moment, when all seemed good with the world that he entered like a tornado.

16

Pumpkin and Baby!

'Pumpkin!' the man wailed dramatically as he rushed past me to Ananya's bed and wrapped his long arms around her.

'Why does this man look familiar?' I thought to myself as I observed the back of the man who held Ananya in a tight embrace. The next instant it hit me like a bolt of lightning. I almost died of shock right there and then.

'Pita ji!!!!!' I said horrified!

What the hell!

'Ohh...Kasturi!' said Pita ji turning around for a second and speaking as if it was most natural for us to meet while he was passionately hugging my roommate.

'Baby,' said Ananya softly looking at Pita ji with unmistakable tenderness in her eyes. For a second the room swam in front of my eyes.

I turned to look at Ananya and what I saw shocked me. She had the same weak simpering look on her face as she had when she was on those clandestine calls with 'mummy'.

'Mummy!' said Varun triumphantly thinking in the same fashion as I did, 'this is mummy, Pita ji is mummy!!' he finished dramatically jabbing a finger at Pita ji. Yes, so Pita ji is indeed mummy. And that is one sentence I never thought I would say.

'Mummy!' I thought now furiously thinking about my own mother. Just yesterday she had spent hours on the phone trying to convince me to meet Pita ji again as she thought he was a really good 'catch'. He was one of the nicer guys we had found and she was sure he would make a very good husband. Yeah right!

But, wait a second. What is this? How? When? Where?

'Will someone explain?' said Varun. Telepathy. Mind twin, this guy, Varun. I think, he speaks.

The love birds who were in a deep, passionate embrace reluctantly parted.

'Kas, Varun, I am sorry you guys found out this way...,' said Ananya in that now familiar croak of hers. Pita ji was standing next to her holding her good hand. I think he had tears in his eyes. Ugghh.

'We have been seeing each other for some time now guys...I wanted to tell you both but we did not know how Kasturi would react. Please Kas, I went ahead only because I was sure that you did not like him that way at all...,' said Ananya, her voice trembling. I could make out that she was finding it difficult to pick the right words. Pita ji stood quietly just looking at his injured beloved with tearful eyes and a pained expression.

'That's why I called you guys on Saturday when all this happened,' continued Ananya, 'I wanted to tell you both...but I could not because of course I got rammed into by an auto...I am sorry...really...really...sorry guys,' said Ananya looking down.

'So you guys met through me?' I said still not sure, 'when I had taken Ananya to keep me company for my second "date" with Pita ji?'

'Of course! And did you not see it? We hit off like crazy...I love him more than I ever thought I could love anyone...,' simpered Ananya transforming into a lovey-dovey somebody I did not know at all.

'Pumpkin...don't speak...you will get tired...' crooned Pita ji placing a concerned hand on her shoulder.

'Ok, baby, whatever you say,' agreed Ananya with a rather pious, obedient look on her face.

Pumpkin and Baby?! Oh well. I started feeling a little faint.

Ananya kept looking at me, her eyes questioning and begging for approval. My face was expressionless. Varun, as usual, had his mouth open.

'Kasturi, please say something,' said Ananya looking at me with unsure eyes. I could sense how much she wanted me to say that it was all ok. She waited nervously for the stamp of my approval.

'It's ok, pumpkin,' I said my face breaking into a grin. After all what problem could I possibly have if my best friend had found someone she really loved? Though of course why anyone would fall in love with Pita ji remained a mystery to me. Apart from that I was more than happy with the turn of events.

Pita ji grinned. 'You are a champ, Kas!' he said as if he and I knew each other since we were knee high. I grinned at him.

Varun finally shut his mouth but opened it soon enough to join in all the grinning that was going around.

'I am absolutely fine with the whole thing guys! If you are happy, what more could I want?' I said, ' however I have one condition...,' I added threateningly.

'What?' asked Ananya.

'I will still call Amay, Pita ji,' I said.

Pita ji laughed.

'Sure, I give you that permission!' he said good naturedly. Now that I had no danger of ever getting married to Pita ji, I immediately took a liking to his easy smile and open persona. I grinned at him.

'Hi, I am Varun,' said Varun walking up to Pita ji and offering his hand, 'I must say I have heard a lot about you. It is nice to finally meet you!' he added politely. I grinned further as I realised that all that Varun had heard about Pita ji were the abuses I had used repeatedly to describe him.

'Hi, I am, as you know, Pita ji. And I must also say that I have heard a lot about you. It is nice to finally meet you too,' said Pita ji as we all laughed politely at Pita ji's lame attempt at humour.

'Guys, thank you for taking care of Anu. I just came back from London. I have been fretting ever since I could not get through Anu's phone and have been worried sick since I found out about her accident... I landed today morning and all this while have been thanking god for the two of you,' he said sincerely. Varun and I looked at each other and then at him.

'We love your pumpkin, yaar,' said Varun smiling and coming closer to Pita ji.

'She would do the same for us...,' I added shrugging. Really, I believed that. What else are friends for if not to help when needed?

Pita ji smiled at us, a genuine smile full of gratitude and then turned around to devote full attention to Ananya. The two sat together for a long time. Pita ji was interested in knowing every little detail about every big tiny injury on Ananya's body. No matter how gory the detail, he wanted to hear it and feel Ananya's pain. The two of them held hands all the while.

Pita ji and his Pumpkin.

Pumpkin and her Baby.

'God bless them,' I thought angelically to myself as I turned to go out of the room to give the lovie-doveies some privacy. As I pirouetted, my heels cracked and I crashed full body into Dolly, the nurse who was carrying a tray with loads of glass bottles containing suspicious looking yellow fluid. I fell on her, with her, and as we fell together – the 50 kgs of me and the 150 of her – the gazillion bottles crashed around us spilling the yellow fluid all over us and around us. The stench that engulfed me seconds later dispelled any doubts that I might have had about the origins of the yellow fluid.

I was on all fours and apologising furiously in every direction when I heard someone clear his throat. I looked up to see Pita ji's face poking out from in between the drawn curtains of Ananya's room. He was shaking his head with the expression of a father disappointed yet again by his favourite child.

At that moment I went back to hating him.

Huh!

17

Komal has Fur

17 July 2009

10.00 p.m.

Rajeev sir has gone to Chandigarh for some office work and I decided to spend the night with Pumpkin. Pita ji is now a constant presence in the hospital room, he seems to be on indefinite leave from work and has devotedly glued himself to Ananya's bedside.

There is not an iota of doubt that Pita ji and Anu are a sickeningly overtly romantic couple. Yet there is something about them as a couple that I find incredibly endearing. What they share seems to be very innocent and pure. With Ananya sick, the *pita* in Pita ji has awoken with a vengeance like never before.

'One more spoonful, Pumpkin,' crooned Pita ji, sitting on Ananya's bed with a bowl of horrible hospital soup in his hands.

'No baby, I cannot drink any more,' pouted Ananya.

'For my sake, Pumpkin,' pleaded Pita ji. Ananya looked helpless. How could she possibly say no to anything that had to be done for Pita ji's sake?

'Okay, only for you,' she said as she opened her mouth wide. It was then that I decided to take my leave. I had seen enough of the insides of Ananya's mouth for a life time now. I walked quietly towards the canteen thinking about Purva. It had not escaped my attention that ever since Purva had met Rajeev sir, I had never gotten a chance to see him alone. In fact, he had reduced the number of his visits to Ananya's room by half and was sending Dr Ajay in his place more often than ever before. It was at that moment that I saw Dr Ajay walk across the corridor.

'Hello doc,' I called out to him.

'Hey Kasturi, how are you?' said Dr Ajay.

'Am good, thank you. Can you please tell me where I can find Dr Purva?'

'Anything wrong with Ananya?' he asked immediately alert.

'No no,' I hurriedly told him, 'I just wanted to speak to Dr Purva.'

'Oh...well he is not on duty...you can check in the library...the tables at the back, he is generally there. By the way is Varun around?' he asked.

I thanked him for the information, answered his question and made my way to the library. I had been there before when Purva had taken me on a guided tour of the hospital. I sighed as I reminisced those days. Purva was decidedly friendlier then. I felt an incredible urge to speak to Purva, to clear out the air in between us. What was going on in his mind? Could I help in any way? The multitude of questions tormented me in a quiet yet painful way as I walked to the library. I was acutely aware that all was not OK between us and I wanted desperately to change it.

I made my way to the back of the huge AIMMS library and had no difficulty in spotting him. He was slumped over a fat book, fast asleep, a pen clutched in his hand.

I stood there for some time, in the silent, mostly deserted library, watching him sleep. He looked calm and, even in his sleep, responsible. I stared at his scars for some time and wondered about the night that gave him those. I have never met anyone whom I have felt so grateful to, whom I have grown to admire so much...may god bless him, I thought to myself. After a few more minutes, I turned around and quietly made my way out of the library.

18 July 2009

Ma called up to ask me why I was not showing more interest in Amay. Apparently she has been talking to his parents each day and both sets of parents think that we are a couple made in heaven. She has suggested that I spend more time with Pita ji and maybe go for a movie or a romantic candlelight dinner. In case Amay is not showing adequate interest, Ma has suggested that I start wearing really short skirts.

What she does not know is that I spend time with him almost each day, while he coochie-cooes with the love of his life. What I would not give for her to find that out.

19 July 2009

'Do you think I should talk to my folks about Rajeev sir?' I asked the three people sitting in front of me.

'No,' said Pita ji.

'No,' said Varun.

'No,' croaked Ananya.

'Why?' I asked surprised.

'How can you be so naïve Kas? You hardly know him! Has he asked you to marry him?' questioned Ananya.

'No...,' I said suddenly feeling a little stupid.

'Then shut up and don't involve your parents in this, you will mess it up for yourself!' she warned.

24 July 2009

As I walked down the hospital corridor replying to a hopelessly romantic text from Rajeev sir, I looked up to see Dr Purva walking in the other direction.

'Purva!' I shouted.

'Hey hi!' he said walking towards me.

'How are you?' I asked him trying to strike up a conversation though I really did not even know what I wanted to say! Before Purva could answer, my cell beeped the receipt of a message. I quickly opened the message to check Rajeev sir's reply.

'Can't wait to spend the rest of my life in your arms,' it read.

Bleh! He can be so very corny sometimes I thought as I felt the now familiar blush creep up my cheeks. There were three smileys at the end of the message.

'How is Rajeev?' asked Purva breaking my line of thought.

'He is doing good, thanks,' I said formally.

'Umm...so you guys are seeing each other?' he asked hesitatingly as we started walking together.

'I guess...kind of.'

'Oh,' he said his face devoid of any expression. I searched his face for approval but did not see anything. We were both quiet for some time as we walked on.

'Why are you meeting boys for marriage then?' he asked.

'My mother is forcing me to...but I have started seeing Raeev sir only recently, I was not going out with him when I met you...and I am not meeting any more guys right now...,' I blabbered trying to explain things to him.

'Hey...relax Kasturi...,' he said putting a comforting arm on my hand, ' I am happy for you,' he added smiling now.

I smiled.

'Thanks,' I said.

'Only thing is if I knew I had limited time to impress you I would have tried a little harder,' he winked at me as he said that.

Although he winked and I laughed it off why was it that I could not shake off the feeling that there is more to Purva's feelings about me than what meets the eye? Anyways, maybe I am thinking too much. I am going to send Rajeev another message and put two virtual kisses in it. Oh! How I love doing this.

2 August 2009

I was sitting next to Ananya's hospital bed when a policeman entered the room without knocking – six feet tall, dark, wrathful eyes and a fierce mouth. He was carrying what looked like an AK-47, ready to shoot any and every one.

'Kasturi ji?' he asked in an almost feminine voice looking around like a little lost child with big moustaches. Varun giggled and I immediately felt more at ease.

'Yes,' I said weakly.

'The sketch artist is here Kasturi ji. I hope you remember the details of the auto driver's face, baby ji,' he said smiling nervously. Baby ji! I rolled my eyes.

Oh yeah. How exciting. I thought Ananya's mother had forgotten all this. She had been visiting us quite often in the hospital and I had been witness to quite a few ugly fights between mother and daughter.

'Yes, I remember his face,' I said as that dark angry looking face flashed in my head.

I was then taken to the doctor's room where a meek looking man was waiting with some canvas like thing and pencils. I started off very nervously quite unhappy about getting involved in such stuff but I started feeling better as I realised that the sketch artist seemed more scared than I was. A few minutes into the session, from the corner of my eye I saw the familiar broad and tall physique of Dr Purva materialise at the door. He stood there for some time but did not come in.

'Is all ok?' he whispered to the *chapraasi* outside the door.

'Ji, sir.'

'Please let me know if there is any problem, I am in this ward,' he said pointing somewhere nearby, 'keep an eye on Kasturi if she needs anything.'

My heart warmed to Purva. Once again.

4 August 2009

I realised today that I am getting a pretty decent salary for stealing glances at my boss when not texting him sweet nothings.

Who can ask for a better job profile?

7 August 2009

7.00 p.m.

Most unbelievably, I am yet again getting ready to meet another guy. This is why I need to tell mum about Rajeev sir. This 'meet-a-different-boy-each-second' madness has to stop!

8.00 p.m.

To give the details, I have once again been cornered into this situation by my mother who reiterated yet again all she has done for me ever since I was born and how I have turned into an emotionless girl with no gratitude for people who have made her who she is today.

I remedied matters by immediately bursting into essential tears making my mother think that I was deeply hurt by what she had said thereby making her feel much better. As an absolutely inconsequential by-product of the whole fight with ma, I am sitting here again, in Pizza Hut, waiting for some random guy called... called ...errr...oh my god!

Okay! Great! So I don't even know the name of the guy I have come all the way to meet. Why do such things happen to *me*?

8.10 p.m.

I cannot recall his name! I have spoken to him once over the phone and of course he had introduced himself but I was not really listening. This was so because Rajeev sir who was sitting next to me was trying to make me giggle by tickling me unto death. So not really my fault. Apart from that I have received a few emails from him, so obviously I have seen his name. It's just that he will now come any minute and I cannot for the life of me, recall his name.

8.11 p.m.

I have messaged mum asking her to tell me his name.

8.12 p.m.

Mum has replied saying that she also does not know his name. She has forwarded my message to dad who she says might remember the name.

8.13 p.m.

I have replied asking her what kind of a mother she is. She does not even know the name of the guy who she thinks can be her only son-in-law.

8.14 p.m.

Mum has helpfully provided me with the names of the boy's mother, father, grandfather, chacha ji, sister, chachi ji and pet dog. The pet dog is, by the way, called Tommy which is just so banal and unoriginal.

8.15 p.m.

I replied by asking mum why exactly she thinks that knowing the name of the family dog is going to help matters at hand.

8.16 p.m.

Mum has replied very wisely and profoundly saying that something is better than nothing.

10.00 p.m.

I was about to reply to mum's wisecracks when I saw him enter. The photograph attached to his bio data at least ensured that I was actually able to recognise him.

I stood up as he approached my table. He was tall and thin with a thin moustache outlining his lips. He seemed like the kind of guy who would run and tell his mother if I was not polite enough with him.

'Kasturi,' he said, looking at me from top to toe.

'Hi…I am Kasturi,' I said hoping that he might take his own name in response.

But he did not.

'Hi, yes, of course I know your name,' he said as if it was impossible to actually meet someone whose name you did not know. Ahem. When in doubt just smile and that is exactly what I did, I smiled my widest.

After shaking hands we both took our seats. As he put his elbow on the table and stroked his chin with his arm, I noticed the most fascinating thing about him that had so far escaped my attention. He was exceptionally hairy! By exceptionally hairy I mean that he was pretty much the hairiest guy I had ever set my eyes on. In fact from what I could see and analyse, it just was not possible to be hairier than him. In fact it was not hair, it was fur that covered him.

His arms seemed to be covered in a blanket of the aforementioned black fur. I openly stared at his arms for a few seconds. My eyes travelled to his collar bone from where as expected I could see the start of another dark blanket under his shirt, bursting to escape free.

I almost threw up mentally. Whom does my mother want me to marry?

'So, tell me something about yourself?' he said sounding very enthusiastic.

'There is not much to tell,' I replied almost apathetic to his query.

He smiled indulgently.

'So you are looking for a suitable boy for marriage.' he tried again.

Who speaks like that, I thought to myself? Suitable boy for marriage? Ewks!

'No, I am not, my parents are,' I replied curtly.

'Awww...come on,' he said very patiently as if humouring a sulking ten year old. I think he imagined a halo develop around his head and wings sprout out of his hairy shoulders as he dived deep into the role of the kind, patient man dealing with a difficult girl.

'It's OK...I know girls don't like to meet guys for marriage purposes. Especially highly qualified girls like you, ma'am.' The halo deepened in colour and the wings became bigger.

I nodded my head, feeling rebellious at his patience. I wondered what more I would have to endure for 'marriage purposes'!

'You know, I'm reminded of a song when I look at you,' he said in a soft voice. He stared at me with a dreamy, faraway look in his eyes.

In spite of myself, I immediately felt interested. No one has ever ever ever sung a song for me! I looked at him and said 'Which one?'

He cleared his throat. I waited with baited breath for whateverhisnameis to start singing. There were a gazillion songs about beauty that came to my mind. I blushed as I wondered which one whateverhisnameis would pick.

'*Kasturi methi, degi mirach! Asli masale! Sach! Sach! MDH! MDH!*' he sang in a melodious, loud voice.

I sat still for a few minutes once he had finished. I had to pinch myself. I could not really believe that this had happened.

In each individual's life there is a distinct, life changing moment, the kind of event that totally alters the path life has been taking till then. For me it was the day when this MDH jingle was aired on tv. To this day I recall with a shudder the next day in school. During lunch time all the boys in class surrounded me and sang that song till I started bawling my head off and someone went and told Miss Jacobs, my class teacher about what was happening. Miss Jacobs had to leave her lunch and beat up at least fifteen boys before they stopped singing. One of my friends from school still has a scar from the beating he got that day from Ms Jacobs. Boys from my class have physical scars from the memory, I have emotional scars from it.

I grimaced. Someone sitting at a table close by giggled. I grimaced further and felt hot on my cheeks.

'*Bhaloo* sings well,' some cool dude from the same table commented loud enough for both of us to hear.

My chance to giggle and whateverhisnameis's turn to grimace.

I think he saw me giggling and that angered him further. The halo and the wings all but disappeared in a jiffy. In typical Delhi-hot-headed guy fashion, he got up angrily and headed towards that table to settle scores with the guy who had complimented his singing while referring to him as *bhaloo*, to which might I, in all objectivity add, whateverhisnameis did bear a significant resemblance to.

What followed this was something, the memory of which will make me cringe for the rest of my life.

Seeing things heat up, in a hopelessly filmy manner, I also got up, rushed to whateverhisnameis' side and planted myself between him and the cool dude. The two men stood there, breathing fire with each man looking more belligerent than the other one. Furthermore, I put a hand on whateverhisnameis's chest and said, 'Please don't do anything, please.' I could feel hair under the shirt. I will not forget the feeling for a long time to come.

The two men glared at one another for a minute, but then whateverhisnameis relaxed. Seeing that, the other guy relaxed as well and major tragedy was averted. I breathed a sigh of relief.

'Keep your *bhalu* chained,' the other guy sneered at me as he turned around to leave.

Whateverhisnameis left in a huff soon after without an apology of any kind leaving me to settle the bill. As I saw his retreating back his name hit me like a bolt of lightning.

Komal. Komal Sharma. That is his name. I giggled to myself as I wondered about the contradictions in life.

18

The Grand Plan and
the Daughter of India

9 August 2009

I cannot go around meeting boys like this when I know I love
Rajeev sir so much. Maybe it is time I tell my folks about us.
Dad is already a little suspicious about Rajeev sir and has told me
that he thinks I speak more about him than is required.

10 August 2009

10.00 p.m.

I just came back from India Gate where I spent three hours with
Rajeev sir. We walked around the monument talking and eating
ice creams. All the while we held hands — just like couples in
love always do. I like the way his hand feels around mine. And
I absolutely love it when he puts his arm around my waist.

He was looking so absolutely, devastatingly, handsome and I
wondered for the nth time why he has chosen me when he could

have gotten someone at least a hundred times prettier. I could see several girls turning their heads to have another look at him. It made me feel proud and small at the same time.

I love the pink of his lips, the brown of his eyes and the dimple of his cheeks. I love him, love each bit of him. I love my Rajeev sir. I love him for the gentleman that he is, I love him for the playful monkey that he can often be.

12 August 2009

8.00 p.m.

'Beta?'

Oh no! The sugary sweet voice! DANGER!

'Ma?'

'Keep Saturday free...' she said sweetly.

'Why?' I said very very suspiciously.

'Beta, you know Amay, whom you so disrespectfully call Pita ji...,' she added helpfully.

'Yes?'

'Well, his mother and father want to meet you!' she said coyly as if she was talking of her own marriage. I could hear her smile. Oh, wait what did she just say? WHAT?

'W-H-A-T,' I said shocked out of my wits. You could have knocked me down with the proverbial feather at that moment.

'Well...they say Amay likes you and so they want to take things further...' she said slowly and shyly as if giving me good news, 'Beta, you must wear a salwar-kurta and keep your hair open. Your daddy and I will also come so that we can meet Amay's parents as well...they are such nice, rich people...' she rambled on.

I had stopped listening quite some time back.

Bloody hell.

BLOODY HELL.

8.06 p.m.

'Where is HE?' I thundered on the phone call that Ananya picked up. I knew they were at the hospital and Pita ji would be by Ananya's side.

'Where is who?'

'Pita ji!! Who else?' I thundered ready to explode with anger.

I could hear Ananya putting me on speaker mode and calling 'sugar' to take the call.

'Hey Kas!' said Pita ji happily.

'Pita ji!' I said murderously.

'What happened Kas?' he asked in the most calm, casual voice ever.

'What the hell did you tell your parents?' I thundered again.

'Well they were asking me what I had for lunch and I told them I had had Maggie to which Mamma said that I should eat rotis more often as it is good for the bowels to which I said that...'

'What-did-you-tell-your-parents-about-me,' I said slowly now seething with rage. How did they take this guy in ISB? I mean like...what...how?

'Oh no! What did they do?'

Oh so he finally gets the drift, does he?

'They want to see me! Meet me! See if I can be their daughter-in-law! Your wife!' I screamed helplessly.

'Sheesh,' said Pita ji.

I heard Ananya gasp.

'What did you tell them?' I pestered.

'Yaaar...it must be my fault...,' he said slowly.

Ananya gasped yet again.

'What? You want to marry Kasturi?' croaked Ananya, shocked.

'Oh no pumpkin...no...no...no...you have it wrong,' crooned Pita ji.

I groaned as I heard Ananya start sniffing, followed by the sound of shuffling of feet as Pita ji moved closer to Ananya.

'No baby no...just hear me out,' he crooned yet again.

'For god's sake, will someone tell me what the hell is going on?' I shouted into the phone.

'Okay. Now Kas, be patient. See Ananya's mom won't agree to us getting married...,' said Pita ji as if that explained the need of getting married to me!

'So? You know that I love Rajeev sir to death!'

'Of course! But not more than I love Anu,' he said in that dreamy voice I had still not managed to tolerate for more than two seconds. I wanted to slap Pita ji right away.

'Please shut up!' I said through gritted teeth as I got more and more frustrated by the second.

'Okay...so...we need more time. My folks are putting more pressure on me for marriage and I thought if I said that I found you okay...they would get busy with you and I will get some time to convince Anu's mom,' he explained. I noticed how his voice shuddered as he uttered the last two words of the sentence. For once, I could understand. Having Ananya's mom for a mom-in-law, life really could not get more dangerous than that!

'Cool! Works fine for you. But what about me?' I said aghast at his lop sided, self-centred logic.

'Simple. Let's meet my parents, then you can be very rude, parents will say no, I will say yes, they will say no and I will say that if they cannot allow me to marry a girl they chose in the first place, they might as well go to hell and let me choose a girl on my own. Enter Anu,' he said with a flourish.

I had this strong urge to get in the phone, get out of the other end, roll some newspaper and thwack that bloated head of his that certainly contains trash instead of a brain.

'Are you mad?' my voice was quiet with rage.

'Why? What's wrong?' he said sounding surprised.

It was one of those moments when I wondered, yet again, what Ananya saw in Pita ji.

'Okay, so I go make an ass of myself in front of your parents and mine. You two get time, great. But what happens to me? My mom will kill me for misbehaving in front of your parents!'

'Chill...you get time too. You tell your folks that if these are the kind of potential in-laws they can find for you, then you were better off finding some guy for yourself! Simple.'

I paused.

Hmm...

Not bad.

Not bad at all. My anger subsided. This plan could really work very well.

'By the way, could you not have discussed it with me once before you asked your parents to meet me?'

I could hear him smile.

'That's my issshhhhtlye,' he said. I imagined a cock all feathered and bloated.

'My peachy baby,' crooned Ananya, in the background, like a proud mother hen.

'Pumpkin,' crooned Pita ji.

I rolled my eyes but could not help but smile.

13 August 2009

8.30 p.m.

'Hmm,' said Rajeev sir thoughtfully.

I looked at his handsome face. I saw his eyes follow an attractive looking girl walking past us. We were again standing near India Gate, the sky was dark shade of inky blue with stars twinkling all over. We then sat, a little away from the crowd, behind a huge tree that formed a natural, dark green canopy. One of my hands was entwined in Rajeev sir's and in the other I held a stab of corn both of us had been sharing.

There were lots of people walking or sitting at a little distance from us. There were couples like us, parents with kids and grandparents with their grandchildren. In spite of the beauty that life spread around me, all I could think of was Pita ji's grand plan. What if something went wrong?

'So...what do you think I should do?' I asked Rajeev pulling his face closer to mine.

I had just told Rajeev of Pita ji's plan in detail. I was unsure about how Rajeev would react to it.

'I think you should tell your parents about us,' he said calmly after a moment's pause.

My eyes widened with surprise as he finished the sentence and looked at me smiling. I stood up. He stood with me.

'Shut your mouth, sweetheart,' he said smiling as he brought to my kind notice that my mouth had been open since he had uttered the sentence a few seconds back.

'What...err...I mean...what do you want me to tell my parents,' I said still not sure. My heart started thumping loudly.

'That we love each other and would like to spend the rest of our lives together!' he said simply.

I stared at him not able to utter a word.

'Oh...I mean...,' he suddenly looked unsure, 'would you like to wait...I mean like if you are not sure then of course...I would understand and would be ready to give us more time,' he said hesitatingly.

Under the inky blue of the sky and the dim roar of cars whishing by, tears filled my eyes blurring the one face I loved more than any other. I could not believe what I was hearing. I had dreamt of this moment ever since I had first set eyes on Rajeev sir and now when this was actually happening, I did not know what to do. Bumbling, stammering me and the suave, confident Rajeev sir? What a pair we will make!

The next second I found myself in his arms, hugging him as tight as I could! Was this really happening?

Rajeev sir drew me apart, held my face in his hands and held me at a hand's distance. All I could see was the brown of his eyes.

'Marry me,' he said kissing my forehead and dispelling any doubts I might have ever had about his intentions.

It was not a question. An answer was not expected. It worked well for me as my throat was all tight and happy tears had started their journey southwards. Marry him? Marry him and be his wife? And spend the rest of my life looking into those pools of warm chocolate? Marry him?

Mrs Rajeev Mehrotra. That's going to be me! Mrs Rajeev Mehrotra! I cannot believe that Rajeev sir has actually asked me to marry him.

I spent the rest of the evening with a goofy grin plastered right across my face.

20 August 2009

7.00 p.m.

Just to recapitulate my predicament for the sake of posterity: I am madly in love with a colleague from office who looks like the proverbial Greek God. My parents, however, know nothing about it. My boyfriend and I have just decided to get married of which again, my parents have no idea. Even though I claim to be madly in love with one guy, I am now going to meet the parents of another guy who is one, a good friend of mine whom, interestingly enough, I cannot tolerate for more than a minute and two, is madly in love with my best buddy from office.

Oh well…such things happen in everyone's life, don't they?

7.01 p.m.

God, please please can you help me?

7.02 p.m.

No, I think this might be too tough for even god to sort out.

7.03 p.m.

Am I having a heart attack?

7.04 p.m.

No, not a heart attack, I think this is just an anxiety attack. I should get used to these, should not I?

7.05 p.m.

I might die.
I think I will.

7.06 p.m.

I am sure I will.

22 August 2009

Rajeev sir now calls me the 'future Mrs Mehrotra'. I blush each time he does that.
Kasturi Shukla Mehrotra. I am dying to be her. There is one teeny little problem. I don't see how my mum would ever agree to the match. Rajeev sir is not a Brahmin boy, you see.

24 August 2009

8.00 a.m.

I am supposed to meet Pita ji's parents tomorrow. I have not been eating since yesterday. I am anxious and keep having palpitations. I might die of a sudden heart attack. I think I need to see a doctor.

4.00 p.m.

Rajeev sir sent me a text saying that he cannot wait for the day he and I will be man and wife.
Swoon

25 August 2009

10.00 a.m.

'Pita ji,' I barked into the phone having come out of the office building for the tenth break since nine o'clock when I had come to office. The *chai wala* near by dropped his sieve and glared at me.

'Yes!' he said in whisper.

'I just wanted to tell you how much I hate you right now,' I said.

'That's ok, sweetie, I know that,' he said sweetly.

'I hate you. I hate you. I hate you,' I said loudly into my phone.

'I know, sweetie, I love you too. See you later, bye,' Pita ji said cheerfully.

Hell.

12.00 noon

'I do not know how to be rude!' I wailed into the phone.

'Honey, no! You are quite good at it, don't worry. You will be fantastic. You can be so rude!' said Ananya in an attempt to comfort me. However, I did not feel too happy with the statement.

She is still in hospital but is recovering at a marvelous speed. Her doctors are very happy with the rapid progress she had made in the last few days.

3.00 p.m.

I just got an 'all the best' message from Purva. I could imagine him smiling broadly to himself as he would have typed the message. I know for a fact that he finds my situation very funny.

6.00 p.m.

I was forced to spend two hours at a beauty parlour. Ms Rose, the lady at the parlour, tried her best to make me look fairer and prettier. After paying ₹1,500 to her and obediently smiling and blushing when all her staff agreed that I looked really beautiful, I went to the bathroom and scrubbed all the makeup off my face. My face was red with all the scrubbing.

6.30 p.m.

Mum, dad and I waiting at 'Punjabi by Nature' to meet Pita ji and his parents. Thanks to my scrubbing right after Ms Rose and her staff had done their work, Mum has about ten times more makeup than I do. Mum is wearing her heaviest sari and has three gold necklaces around her neck, as if that would certainly dig out a YES from Pita ji's parents. Little does she know what the evening has in store for her.

Poor mum.

6.31 p.m.

And the drama begins:

So in came Pita ji's mom, dad, chachi ji, chacha ji, younger cousin, some elderly relative and Pita ji's nani ji a much revered elder of the clan. As Pita ji and his family walked into the restaurant in a weirdly perfect file, my mother expressed an immense amount of surprise and enthusiasm.

After a multitude of pleasantries and exclamations and a lot of hustle and even more bustle, we all sat down around a table arranged in the centre of the restaurant. Then followed the obligatory round of compliments where everyone except me was complimented for something by someone.

I had been smiling stupidly trying to look like the bride to be but so far everyone had been religiously ignoring me at which I felt oddly hurt and ignored. Was not I supposed to be the centre of all attention now? I was lost in these thoughts when suddenly, Pita ji's mother who was sitting opposite to me lunged the whole distance between us and putting her hand on my chin, said, 'What a sweet little girl our Kasturi is.'

To which my mother tittered and said, '*Arre* so is Amay any less?' As an afterthought, she also lunged forward and touched Pita ji's chin.

Pita ji squirmed, Pita ji's mom smiled and dad and I exchanged a look.

'So beta, what do you do?' asked Pita ji's mummy ji.

I was thinking of something slightly rude to say, when mum answered on my behalf, 'MBA from one of the best B-schools in the country. Just like bhaiya here,' she said pointing yet again to Pita ji.

The whole group nodded its head in agreement.

The topic then moved to how girls were getting as much education as boys and how in so many fields they were actually doing a much better job. Everyone agreed with everyone. Every one smiled at everyone.

Pita ji's mom complimented my mother's sari. Mom immediately complemented Pita ji's mom's sari which led to a discussion on how some women have the knack of choosing the right saris while others just cannot find a single decent one. Both women agreed that both of them belonged to the former category.

Nani ji, not getting enough attention, cleared her throat and asked me if I said my prayers daily.

'No, not at all,' I said grabbing the opportunity with glee and delight.

'No?' repeated Nani ji horrified that such a person could actually exist on this planet.

'No?' repeated Pita ji's mummy ji. If all the bahus in *Kyuki Saas Bhi Kabhi Bahu Thi* are religious and pray to god three times a day then it would be nothing short of sacrilegious if her bahu did not tread the same path of goodness and virtue.

'No...No...' chirped my mum, 'but she goes to the temple each Monday and Thursday. She also fasts every Tuesday for a good husband.

My mum looked all pious and holy herself as she sat there with her hands folded. Of course, I neither go to the temple each Thursday nor have I ever fasted on a Tuesday.

'Oh...very nice...very nice,' said Nani ji smiling now. A girl who willingly goes to the temple twice a week can obviously be forced into praying daily, Nani ji must have thought.

The tense moment had now passed and everyone relaxed.

'See, my daughter never lies...' said my mother patting my head and smiling sweetly.

My dad and I exchanged yet another look. Dad sighed.

Food ordered in huge quantities was brought in soon. Mom heaped mountains of food loads into each person's plate and insisted that everyone has another helping of everything.

Pita ji's chachi's daughter was the only one who openly stared at me. She refused to take her eyes off me for even a second during the meal. So when no one was looking at us, I made a face at her. She retaliated by sticking out her tongue at me at the exact minute nani turned to ask her for something. That led to the horrified nani ji scolding the poor girl in front of everyone. I grinned to myself. Pita ji glared at me.

So, in general Pita ji looked decidedly more uncomfortable than I was. My cell beeped. It was a message from Pita ji.

'Love you Pumpkin!' it read.

'I am not your pumpkin, idiot!' I replied immediately having understood that the message was for Ananya. Pita ji's cell beeped as he received my message.

A few seconds later mine beeped again.

'Sorry sorry, you just look so much like a pumpkin right now in that swollen salwar-suit – my fingers could not resist.'

'Idiot! Get lost,' I replied immediately.

Pita ji's chachi raised her voice over the humdrum of polite conversation that I had lost track of in the last few minutes, 'Do you guys see what is happening here?' she asked of everyone in general and no one in particular.

All faces turned towards her. She seemed particularly smug for my comfort.

'Kasturi and Amu! They are busy messaging each other! The love birds are in their own little world! Cannot you hear the message beeps?' she said as she burst into delighted yet unnecessary peals of laughter.

Others at the table joined in as I felt red hot on the cheeks!

'Amuuuuu!!! Love birds!!!' chachi ji squealed as she poked Pita ji in the ribs. I decided that of all the people at the table (including my mum renowned for being really difficult) it was definitely chachi ji I could not stand.

Nani ji for all her *pooja-path* looked ready to have a heart attack as she understood what was happening.

I fumed at Pita ji, 'Pita ji!!' I muttered angrily under my breath shaking my head. It was after all his fault. He should have been more careful! What was the need to message Ananya right now? What's the point in loosing focus when there is so much hanging in such delicate balance?

I saw three faces turn sharply to stare at me the very next moment. Pita ji himself, his pita ji and my pita ji. The table turned quiet. No one said anything for the next few seconds when silence hung heavy. I could not understand why everyone was so shocked. What had gone wrong?

'Babloo beta, Kasturi is speaking to you. Answer her, beta,' said nani ji smiling tenderly both at me and at Pita ji's dad.

I put my hand on my forehead for a second. So, nani ji thinks I am calling Amay's dad Pita ji? As the realisation hit home, I started to feel a little faint.

'Err...yes Beta?' said pita ji's Pita ji a little hesitatingly after a silence of about eight to ten seconds during which no one spoke.

'Ji...why don't you take some more *kadhai paneer?*' I said stupidly, not knowing what to say or do. My answer had a marked effect on people around the table. My mother smiled a jubilant smile, nani ji looked ready to die again, with happiness this time, chachi ji looked smug as she was the one who had caught us love birds red handed and Pita ji's mother looked like she had found her dream daughter-in-law.

Lots of *kadhai paneer* and *naan* later when both parties had dutifully fought over who would pay the bill, nani ji put a hand on my dad's shoulders and said, 'Beta, in this day and age you have brought up a daughter who has such a pure heart that she already considers Amay's father as her own. The credit goes to you beta, for your upbringing. The culture of our great nation is not dead. It lives in parents like you and through you in the daughters of India like Kasturi.'

I had to gulp twice before my throat seemed like it was in working condition. Mom looked around with such a wide grin on her face that I cringed.

The plan had no doubt failed. And as I walked back to the car and tried to save my life as all the women in Pita ji's family decided they wanted to hug the life out of me, I dreaded to think of what would happen next.

19

The Ramifications of a Failed Grand Plan

26 August

5.00 p.m.

As was totally expected, Pita ji's mom called up my mother to tell her that they were hoping to find a daughter-in-law but have, in me, found a daughter who should be a part of their family as soon as the logistics could be arranged. After many filmy dialogues and meaningless giggles, it was agreed that the engagement should be arranged as soon as possible, preferably within the next two months even if that meant that only ten thousand people would be invited. They seemed to be fine with a small gathering.

My mom has been staying with me in Delhi for the last two days and was sitting next to me when she took the call. Needless to add, my mouth went dry when I realised what was happening. Mom put down the phone and turned to me smiling like Cheshire Cat.

'Congratulations on your engagement that will now happen very soon,' she said looking at me with loving eyes.

'What?'

'Yes!' Mom said cheerfully.

'No mom. I cannot marry Amay,' I said. The plan could not have gone more wrong.

'Why? Amay earns 27.5 lakhs a year and you won't have to stay with his parents because he might even shift abroad! He has no siblings, all his parent's property will come to you only,' said mom. All the mentioned reasons are the right reasons to marry any guy, aren't they, I thought ruefully to myself. When will mom learn the basics of love and affection?

'No, Ma,' I said.

'Why? Give me one good reason,' said mom belligerently.

'Because I love someone else,' I said quietly, ready for the storm that I knew would burst in all its fury very soon. This was not how I wanted mom to find out. It was all going horribly wrong. My heart sank further.

Mom remained quiet for a few seconds not really comprehending the full impact of what I had said.

'WHAT?!' screamed Ma once she had figured it out as if the world had come to an end, 'What is his name? Who is he? What is his caste?'

'Rajeev Mehrotra, that's his name. He works with me in office'

'He is not a Brahmin!' screamed mother.

'No, he is not, but so what? I love him!' I screamed back.

'So that is what you have been up to while supposedly working? No wonder girls are simply married off and not allowed to work!

This is what happens if you let your girl loose! She will come back with a Punjabi boy,' mom thundered.

Dad was called up immediately and given the horrific news. Dad tried to calm her down but it was to no avail. A Punjabi boy could not be accepted into the family. I stood dumb struck at mum's superannuated reasoning that came forth in waves.

'How will I ever even look at Preeta didi's face ever again? Her daughters have all married Brahmin boys...no...no...this will just not be allowed Kasturi. You cannot marry the boy,' said mother.

'Mum!' I said helplessly. How does Preeta masi come into the picture, for god's sake!

'No Kasturi, no. Change your job and forget the boy,' Mum said flatly.

'Mum, please, at least meet Rajeev,' I cadged.

'You will see my dead face, Kasturi, if you even take that boy's name in front of me,' said mum looking stone faced as I gasped. Mum has been melodramatic and loud in the past but never so harsh.

I cried nonstop for three hours but mom did not waver. She told me that I can go jump in the river if I want to. She would much rather have a dead daughter than one married out of the caste.

10.00 p.m.

A lot of ugly things have been exchanged between mum and me. I have been crying nonstop and so has mom.

12 midnight

Mom is not sleeping and neither am I. This has to be the worst day of my life. The house seems dark and unhappy. I tried to show mom a picture of Rajeev hoping that his good looks would make mom change her mind. She looked at the framed photograph for a second and then threw it right across the room.

27 August 2009

I took the day off from work. I called up Rajeev and told him about the situation. He offered to come home to discuss this with mom. I told him to come only if he did not fear for his life.

2.00 p.m.

Rajeev sir came home to meet ma. Ma opened the door when the bell rang.

'Yes? Who do you want to meet?' said ma smiling for the first time since I had disclosed my little secret.

'Namaste auntie ji, I am Rajeev. I just wanted to meet you,' said Rajeev sir smiling hesitatingly. I was right behind mom and as I saw Rajeev sir say this I fell in love with him all over again. He looked so innocent and vulnerable standing at my door step, unsure of what my mom would do next.

'Get lost! And don't you DARE show me your face ever again,' screamed my mother as she banged the door shut in his face. My heart broke into a million pieces right then. That was the last straw. How could mom do that to Rajeev sir. How? And why? Just because he is not the same caste? It just strengthened my resolve to marry no one but Rajeev sir. I will also never be able to forgive ma for this. Never ever.

5.00 p.m.

I have been sending apology messages to Rajeev sir. He seems to understand and agrees that the situation is much worse than he had anticipated.

I also messaged Purva, Varun and Pita ji informing them of the latest developments. Purva has asked me not to force anything on mom. She will take time, he says, but who knows she might agree finally.

Purva does not know my mom.

11.00 p.m.

Mom has decided to leave for home early tomorrow morning. She has asked me to not bother with dropping her off to the station. I have been asked not to call her till 'that Punjabi boy' is out of my life and mind.

I have been crying nonstop. Concerned messages from Pita ji, Varun, Purva and Rajeev have been flowing in throughout the day. Pita ji's heartbroken that his plan has landed me prematurely into so much trouble.

28 August 2009

Mom left without even looking at me. Varun came with a taxi to take her to the station. Mom did not even turn her head to say goodbye. I stood there, outside my house at five in the morning with tears streaming down my face. She could hear my broken sobs but she did not turn her head.

29 August 2009

I love Rajeev sir too much. I have made my decision which my mum will view only as contumacious. And the decision is as follows:

I will wait and not hurry into anything but I will not marry anyone except Rajeev sir.

30 August 2009

Rajeev sir and I looked into each other's eyes.

'I love you, sweetie,' he said as his face came closer to mine.

'I love you too,' I said softly.

His eyes smiled into mine as our lips met.

2 September 2009

Ananya's mother is becoming such a big pain now. She made me go to the police station where I gave my evidence. Pita ji and Varun, thankfully accompanied me and refused to leave my side even for a second. It now seems that the guy was actually not just an auto driver but was a small time player in a bigger mafia gang that had so far been operating only in Mumbai.

Great! So now not only do I have a mother who would be happy to see me dead, I also have the mafia who might be happy to grant mum her wish. Oh, is not life lovely?

Anyways, Ananya's mother has promised me that she is watching my back and giving evidence in a discreet way will ensure that no problems arise for me. I am grateful to God for the little mercies in life.

20

The Dummies Guide to Getting Mashed Like a Potato

3 September 2009

'Ananya will be discharged tomorrow,' said Purva smiling at his patient.

It was not unexpected news by any standard but Pita ji squealed like a particularly screechy school girl and clutched Ananya's hand with such force that I was scared it would break again. It would have been particularly funny if it had, by the way.

'You did it Anu, you did it!' said Pita ji pumping his fist in the air. I stared open mouthed.

'I could not have done this without you, sweetie,' said Anu puckering up her face and giving the credit of her success to the man without whom Anu would not have been able to recover. Oh my god. This was just a discharge order coming later than it should have ideally come, not an Olympic gold medal!

I noticed Purva trying to hide his smile as he spent the next few minutes checking Ananya one last time.

'Don't come back anytime soon, except for checkups related to this accident!' said Purva in mock anger. And with that he turned to go. As I stared at Purva's back, it suddenly hit me that this marked the end of seeing Purva on a daily basis. As weird as it may sound but I had gotten very used to having a friend in AIMMS.

'Hey,' I said running to catch up with him as he walked down the hallway.

'Hey,' he said surprised as he turned to face me.

'Can I walk with you for some time?' I asked.

'Yeah of course, Ananya was my last patient for the day. I am now done with the rounds. Want some coffee?' he asked.

I nodded. It was chilly and coffee sounded great at the hour.

We walked together in comfortable silence. I pulled the stethoscope from round his neck, put it around mine and gave him a stern, matronly look while pushing imaginary spectacles up my nose.

He laughed, drawing my attention yet again to his calm and genuine laugh. I smiled to myself amazed at how fond I had become of this quiet, grave looking doctor.

After placing our orders at the counter, Purva and I sat in a quiet corner in the coffee shop. It seemed like an odd night. The air hung heavy over me.

'What are you thinking about, Kasturi?' he asked breaking the silence.

'Nothing special…it's a pretty night,' I said pointing to the dark night outside as equally dark thoughts about mum played havoc in my head. Mom had not taken any of my calls and frankly speaking I was already a little tired of the game now.

'Yes, it is. How is Rajeev?' he asked.

I sighed.

'What do you think of Rajeev, please an honest answer?' I asked inspite of myself. I knew I loved Rajeev but after mum's outburst another angle had emerged. No one in my friend circle had ever said anything nice about Rajeev sir. And while all of them had been very supportive in the last few days no one had said that Rajeev was the right guy for me. They had, I realised, evaded any comment on what they thought about Rajeev. This had been bugging me a little of late.

'That he is a very lucky man,' said Purva almost before I finished my question.

'And why would you think that? Don't you see both of us? He is so good looking and I am the plain Jane,' I said looking down. I was surprised this came out. I had harboured this thought since Rajeev sir had first asked me out. Yet I had not shared this with anyone, not even with Dad.

'Plain Jane?' said Purva from under his eyebrows with a queer smile on his face.

I nodded slowly, my head hung low.

'Let me look at you closely...,' he said, putting on his spectacles and pretending to examine me like a patient. I giggled.

'Hmmm...I see large beautiful black eyes that are intelligent and gentle at the same time...I see a mouth that is always ready to break into a grin...hmm...what else...' he paused and pretended to scrutinise my face more closely, 'I see a slightly upturned nose that might need some plastic surgery in near future...' he said finally.

I pretended to throw his stethoscope at him as he ducked artfully to avoid it.

'OK...OK...I also see someone who cared day and night for her friend with a tenderness and maturity way beyond her years. I see someone who steals trips to the NICU to have a look at the tiny, sick children. I see someone who has made more friends here at AIMMS in the last few weeks than I have in the last couple of years,' he paused and looked at me.

I was looking at him with amazement. How did he know about my all too frequent trips to the NICU and my love for sick children there?

He smiled at me as he read the questions in my eyes.

'I also see someone who speaks kindly to the sweeper. I see someone who orders Chinese food when her sick friend wants to eat it even though she herself hates it,' he continued.

I was again amazed at how he knew that I hated Chinese food. This really had me befuddled. How did Purva know so much about me? There was, however, more and Purva continued speaking.

'I see someone who stays up late into the night sitting by the bed side of her friend working furiously on PPTs and excel sheets for office. I see someone who can laugh easily. I see someone who can make others laugh...I see someone who I love seeing smiling and laughing...,' he trailed off quietly.

I looked down and realised with a start that what he had just said was the most beautiful thing anyone had ever said to me.

'I see a nice, kind girl, Kasturi. Any guy would be lucky to have you love him,' he said quietly. I did not look up.

'...which is why I think Rajeev is a very very lucky man,' he finished in a quiet voice.

There was silence for the next couple of seconds. Both of us were quiet.

I heard a cough. Pita ji.

'Can I join you guys?' he said grinning that goofy smile of his. He was standing a few feet away from us. I wondered how much of Purva's speech he had heard.

'Yes sure,' said Purva smiling.

'Doc, I really need to thank you. I don't know what would have happened if you had not been around,' said Pita ji sincerely.

Purva put his arm around Pita ji, 'It's OK *yaar*... it's my job, plus Ananya is Kasturi's best buddy... don't think about all this, Pita ji,' said Purva giving Pita ji a friendly punch.

I have just realised one important thing. Even sincere, emotional sentences loose their depth and meaning when instead of Amay, Pita ji is called Pita ji.

'I should get going guys... it's past twelve now,' I said suddenly realising that I should have made my move two three hours back.

'I should get back to Ananya,' said Pita ji.

'I will drop you home, it's too late for you to travel alone,' said Purva. At that very instant his pager beeped. He looked at the message and pursed his lips, 'Patient – emergency,' he said looking at me distractedly. Typical Purva, I thought to myself smiling.

'Then I will drop you home,' said Pita ji.

'No guys! I live in Delhi and know this place better than both of you put together! Don't worry, please, I will manage easily. I will call you guys when I reach home,' I said. I dislike this fathering that guys think girls need at all times.

'Take care Kasturi... call me once you reach home,' said Purva as he dashed out to save another life.

As I walked out of the campus of AIMMS, a surprising realisation hit home. I realised that in the last weeks I had grown to absolutely love this place that so fascinatingly saves lives, its buildings that house the million miracles that happen here each day, the nurses who care for strangers, the patients who come here with hopes in their hearts, the doctors who work wonders, Purva.

His words still rang in my head. The intense look in his eyes when he had uttered those words flashed before my eyes. It was so earnest. A look that I had searched for in Rajeev's eyes ever so often but never really found.

Life had changed so much of late, things had become weird. I couldn't guess why these doubts about Rajeev sir had suddenly started cropping up. There was something that I was uncomfortable about even though I could not put a finger on it, there was a nagging doubt that had crept in...Pita ji, Ananya and Purva had all met Rajeev sir and no one had ever said one good thing about him. I mean they had not been impolite in any way but you know how it is, people tell girls how lucky they are to be with the guys they are with. *That* had never happened and I don't know why, but it bothered me. Something was amiss. But then I could not doubt Rajeev in this way. Is this all the strength my love for Rajeev has, I questioned myself?

I felt a little ashamed as the thought crossed my head. Rajeev could have been the jealous boyfriend seeing how much time I spend with Pita ji and how often I speak about Purva, but no, he has always put implicit faith and trust in me. It is wrong of me to think this way. I just need to find a way to get mom to agree to the match. That's all that is needed to make my world perfect again.

But then why is Rajeev never there when I need him the most? When Ananya met with the accident, he was not even reachable by phone...the more I thought about this issue, the more I realised that Rajeev had hardly been around, except on dates when all he wanted to do was hold my hand or hug me or kiss me.

Mad with these thoughts as I made my way, I realised that I had managed to loose my way! So much for knowing Delhi better than Purva and Pita ji put together. But I had just left AIMMS so I could not have gone too far. But it was almost midnight and the road seemed deserted except for a *chai walah* a little distance away and that was a little scary indeed. I could see two men drinking tea at the chai stall. I quickly walked past the *chai walah*, hoping to get onto the main road where there would be more people.

As I took quicker steps, from the corner of my eye, I noticed the men put down their *chai* cups a few seconds after I passed them. Instinctively I felt a little uncomfortable. Something just felt very wrong. Funnily enough, one of the men seemed eerily familiar.

There was no need to panic, I told myself firmly. I took a deep breath and quickened my steps. By this time I was totally lost and had no clue where I was heading. I reached a T-junction of roads. Trusting my luck, I picked the left one and soon found myself on a dark, deserted road almost lined on either side with half built, deserted houses. So much for my luck!

I could hear the footsteps of the men behind me quicken. I turned back to have a look and in that one moment, it so happened that the two men were right below a weak street lamp, the only one I could see for miles.

As the light fell on the two men, blood drained from my face as I stared aghast at one of the men. I had seen those dark frantic eyes before. I had only recently described them to someone in great detail. The man I was facing was the man who had hit Ananya outside the mall.

'Kasturi, no, nothing will go wrong, I am the DM of Arbipur. If I cannot ensure your safety who do you think can?' the haughty voice of Anu's mother promising me safety rang hollow in my ears.

Should I run? I thought to myself.

I did not need to answer as the very next instant, I heard the men break into a run towards me. I kicked off my heels on the side of the road and started running barefoot. I cast one glance at the lovely purple heels I had haggled for hours with the shop owner for and wondered if I would ever set eyes on them again. Then I shook my head and tried to concentrate on the rather important matter – my life was in jeopardy. I had a head start of about a hundred metres. Hundred metres – that was all that was between me and the two men. And the men seemed to be closing in.

I ran wildly, screaming for help, only I am not too sure if any voice was coming out of me. I kept turning back to have a look at the men and I knew they were closing in quicker than I had imagined. I pushed my body harder. In these moments of madness, while externally I was hysterical, my head seemed very calm and seemed to give rational instructions to my body. As I dashed past a house, I even noticed the house number, A/138, my brain recalled with a chuckle that this used to be the house number of a cute neighbour when I was in school and lived with my parents.

I was running and the men were closing in. What could be worse than this? Would these men kill me?

I did not want to find out.

I cast a furtive glance behind my shoulders only to see the men at a hands distance from me. I tried frantically to push myself to run faster. The next instant a cold hand caught my shoulder from behind and roughly yanked me back with such brutal force that I yelped in pain.

'What the hell do you think you are doing?' screamed the auto driver his dirty nails digging into my flesh.

'Let me go!' I screamed as I turned to face the man because of whom Anu had spent weeks in the hospital. The mad eyes stared right back and I felt a shiver down my spine.

The man looked at the other one and laughed, 'We are not letting you go!' he said forcing out his words in a ruthless manner.

The men smelled of cheap alcohol and their eyes had a luscious look that chilled me to my bones. As I struggled to break free, the two men discussed ways to deal with me in a language unfamiliar to me. I had often seen movies where the woman in such a situation hits the man in his groin. I recoiled as the thought crossed my head. It had always made me cringe because whatever the man was up to, it sure would pain like crazy to be hit there. At the moment the auto guy yanked me harder. The next moment I pulled up my feet and mustering up all the strength I had hit him as hard as I could in his groin. This was no time for politeness, I thought grimly.

With shock or pain or maybe both, the auto guy let go his grip of my hand for an instant. Seizing the moment, I turned around and started running back. I could go back to the chai walah I thought. That was the only person I had seen so far. I ran wildly hoping that I was correctly retracing my steps.

'What if the *chai walah* is with these guys?' said a weak voice in my head a moment later. I now recalled that as I had passed the three men, I had heard them chat with the *chai wala* in the same unfamiliar tongue.

And with that my heart sank further. I could not take the risk of running up to the man who was in league with these men.

'No, don't be indecisive, that can even cost you your life. Good or bad, just take a decision,' I told myself fiercely. I was still carrying my bag and sensed my cell vibrate in the side pocket. At the same time my eyes caught sight of the A/138 bungalow a few metres ahead of me. Instinctively, I devised a plan. Vague, yes, but it was better than no plan.

And with that thought in mind, I opened the gate of the deserted house and ran inside the darkness that engulfed the half made structure as fast as my tired legs could carry me.

Once inside the house, I immediately got to work as I knew I had about thirty seconds before the men would barge in. I barely had time to do what I knew was the last chance I would get.

First, I fished out my mobile phone and put it on silent. I resisted the temptation of making a call for help as I knew the men could come in any second and on hearing me speak could drag me to another location before anyone could come for help. No, I had to take this chance. As I pulled out my cell I saw the missed call message flashing on the screen. The missed call was from Purva as I had been praying it would be. Purva's name flashing on the screen, oddly enough, filled me with a sense of calmness. I knew now that he was worried about my whereabouts as I should have called him by this time had I reached home. Someone was worried. Someone knew I was not home, someone knew I was not yet safe. And it was this someone that I was planning to call.

I put the cell on silent and dialled Purva's number. I could hear the call go. I pulled out a shawl from my bag. I wrapped it around the phone, so that the light from the phone would not let my assailants trace me.

The phone light dimmed, just as I heard frantic swearing and knew that the two men had deftly managed to trace me.

As per my plan, I picked up a brick and threw it in the opposite direction.

'Where are you! you $$%^^$#,' shouted one of the men sounding irritated and angry.

I waited for half a second. Please Purva, please I hope you have picked up the phone, I thought frantically.

'Why are you chasing me? Do you want to kill me?' I screamed loudly and hysterically. Too loudly. I did not want Purva to miss a word. Only I did not know if he had even picked up the phone. There was as much chance that he would by now be in the OT with his phone far away from him.

'You are going to give evidence against me in the court for that girl's accident,' said the man.

'So? Why do you want to get into more trouble by hurting me?' I said glad that they seemed interested in a conversation.

The duo remained quiet for a few moments.

'Because, we do more than just go around hitting the daughters of IAS officers,' said one of the men in a low growl. Oh yes, I had no doubt about that one.

I could hear movement. They were following my voice. I was playing a game and I realised that so were they. I picked up the first thing my hand could find in the darkness and threw it in a random direction. I sensed the men move in that direction.

My eyes had adjusted to the darkness inside. Though I was extremely tired with the running, my rational faculty thankfully did not seem to betray at this crucial hour. I was aware of every sound and movement. The basic instinct of survival! I was alone in a dark house with two men in the middle of nowhere in the middle of the night. Only I could save myself.

'Why are you in this house,' I shouted. It was not a stupid question. It was part of my plan.

'Where the hell are you? Don't play with us,' said one, as I heard him curse as he banged into a wall.

'We are in house A/138! It is an empty road but someone close to AIMMS might be walking by, they will probably just have to walk ten minutes in the general east direction to come here. There is a *chai walla* who saw us running. Someone will come and catch you,' I shouted. Purva, please hear all this. Please.

'What is that mad girl blabbering?' said one man.

I repeated as much of the sentence I had just said again. Loud and clear my voice echoed in the in house. I had no idea whether Purva was on the line or not. I was just waiting for a miracle.

'She has a phone!' shouted one man and I heard the two men lunge towards me. I stood there horror struck as I saw my phone blink as someone called. I had the phone behind my back but had no idea of direction. I brought it in front and threw it off in another random direction. I heard the phone hit a wall.

In that split second as I threw the cell away, I had seen who the call was from. Purva.

My heart sank. That meant that he might not have heard anything. The call had probably dropped much earlier.

Great. My last means of communication with the outside world had gone awry.

I started running around madly. There was a lot of commotion and swearing as the two men tried to locate me in the darkness.

Minimum of ten minutes. I had to ward off these men for a minimum of at least ten whole minutes without leaving this house. If Purva had been on the call as I screamed the details, if he had heard all of it, if he had gotten to the part where I had yelled the address, if he could find his way here...my heart sank further as I realised how many ifs there were. And warding off these men for ten minutes seemed to be the most excruciatingly difficult task I had ever embarked upon.

And with that began a murky, parlous game of hide and seek. My mind went back to those locked images of hours spent playing Dark Room with friends and cousins.. I found my body using the same tactics I had learnt as an over enthusiastic dark Room player. *Crouch. Don't breathe too loudly. Lie flat on the floor. Stop breathing when the men were close. No quick movements.* But this brutal game was something different – the dangerous game of shadows. My life was at stake.

I don't know for how long we played this dark game when out of the blue, my foot fell on the broken shards of my mobile phone.

The next instant I yelped in pain and the second after that two pairs of hands had grabbed me; one by my waist and the other by my throat.

In a trance, a few seconds later, I realised that the men were yelling at my face, spitting one invective after the other. One of the men raised his hand and brought in on me with such force that I was blinded by the sheer pain.

'I will kill you!' said the man and I had no doubt about his intention.

The other guy kicked me and yanked my hair. Is this the way I am going to die? I asked myself. Not such a pathetic death? My brain tried to function but my body had no energy left now. I realised with terror that I had given up. I had no plan and I did not even want to think of a way out. I now just wanted these men to kill me as soon as they could.

'This is going to teach you a lesson,' said the auto guy his fetid breath making me cringe as he punched me in the stomach. I tried to concentrate on the images in my head. I could see my class room and my class partner was sitting right next to me. I could see my mum posing for a photograph. I could see Rajeev sir sitting in his cabin and working on a file. I could see Purva laughing. I could see Anu and her injuries. I could hear a car screech to a halt…

What?

What was that noise that I just picked up? One of the men struck me across my face and the other kicked me in my shin. I was now on all fours barely able to even get up. I felt dissociated with my body just vaguely aware of what the men were doing…my brain went back to the unfamiliar images from my childhood that swarmed my head. The holiday in Manali, the mountains, the horse I had petted there, the kitchen guy who made breakfast for us…

I screamed from pain almost involuntarily as yet another hand struck me across my face.

Then it stopped. No, why was not anyone hitting me? Why had it stopped? I looked up as my eyes were blinded by the light from a powerful torch. There were more than the two men now. There was suddenly a lot of activity around me. I spotted a familiar figure going after the auto guy's jugular.

'Purva came…,' and with that last thought that brought unimaginable relief to me, my brain blanked out.

21

The Ramifications of Getting Mashed Like a Potato

6 September 2009

Hazy.

7 September 2009

I can hear some sounds. Someone seems to be calling my name. I try hard to respond but I am not able to. Am I dead?

8 September 2009

When I try to open my eyes I see worried looking men and women in white coats and masks hover around me as machines make weird noises. I can see flowers and birds if I close my eyes.

I think I will not even try to open them again.

9 September 2009

I am somewhere else. It's probably a bigger room and there are fewer machines around me. There is a flower vase next to my bed. And as I closed my eyes I caught a glimpse of my copy of *Villette* next to the flowers. That is my favourite book and I had bought this copy some ten years back.

I feel like reaching out to it and flipping through the pages but my hand does not listen to my brain and my eyes shut again.

Someone kept calling out my name asking me to open my eyes again. The voice belonged to someone I know and I wanted to open my eyes but I could not.

10 September 2009

6.00 a.m.

Some men had punched me? Was that for real or was it just a nightmare? Each time I open my eyes I see Purva sitting next to my bed. There is a huge gash on his face and his arm is in plaster but mainly he looks on at me with worry written across his forehead in bold size 40 font. I want to ask him if the men hurt him too. I try to ask him but no voice comes out of me.

10.00 p.m.

'Kasturi?' a soft voice said.

After much difficulty I was able to open my eyelids. They seemed very heavy.

I saw Purva, Ananya and Pita ji's smiling, relieved faces.

I felt a warm hand softly caressing my forehead. With herculean effort, I tried to look at who the hand belonged to. I was not surprised to see Purva sitting at the head of the bed. I looked at his other hand that was not caressing my forehead. It had a scar running across it. Where had I seen that before? Why was it so familiar? The hand had helped me somewhere before as well. Where? When?

My eyes closed again.

My brain registered that Rajeev's face had not been one of the three peering at mine a few seconds earlier. Thinking so much seemed like a lot of work. My brain shut down again and I drifted into deep sleep.

11 September 2009

1.00 p.m.

I moaned. I felt a searing pain in my hand.

'Kasturi,' a voice said. I tried to open my eyes and this time they opened without too much effort. I saw Anu standing close to me. 'How are you feeling?' she asked looking pale and worried. Her hand was still in a plaster.

'The men?' Where are they?' I mumbled.

'All gone. In jail...,' said Purva coming in from behind Anu. There was a band aid covering up the gash on his face now. His stubble appeared overgrown and he looked like he had not slept in ages.

'Purva,' I called signalling with my fingers asking him to come closer.

'Yes,' he said coming closer. His face was soon a few inches away from mine.

'Thank you,' I said half mouthing the two words.

'Shhh, Kasturi...shhh,' said Purva putting his hand on my head. His eyes looked moist as he caressed my forehead. His hand felt warm and his touch considerate.

'You came...,' I said my voice fumbling and tears gathering in my eyes.

'How could I not?' he said. The simplicity of his four word answer wrenched my heart as tears wet the sides of my pillow. Through my own tears I saw a lone tear stream down Purva's face. I tried to lift my hand to wipe his tear off when I heard Anu give a loud sniff and saw her run out of the room. I could hear her break into tears outside.

12 September 2009

'Why?' I said pointing towards my injuries.

Purva bent closer, 'I don't know,' he said looking very pained, 'I wish I could have come to you earlier,' he said.

'How bad are they?' I asked him wetting my lips with my tongue. My mouth was very dry. Purva got me water and fed it to me with a spoon with a gentleness that I could not ignore.

'Broken hand, hairline fracture and some internal bleeding in the stomach,' he said cringing as if these injuries pained him.

'Will I be ok?' I asked in a broken whisper.

'You *are* okay,' said Purva smiling now.

I tried to smile.

'Rajeev?' I asked.

'He was here....has gone out I guess,' he said.

13 September 2009

I heard someone wailing and generally making a lot of noise. Even before I opened my eyes, I knew it was mum. I gave a mental whoop of joy as I realised that mum with all her antics and theatrics was back!

'Opening! Eyes opening!' she exclaimed as my eyes opened. I had not yet, since my accident, opened my eyes in her presence. She had been, I had been informed, very offended by the preferential treatment my eyes had given to my friends.

'Ma,' I said softly. I could not have put into words the happiness I felt on seeing her back to her old self. She smiled and laughed as she saw me open my eyes. She then went on to hug me so tight that I cried in pain. And then spent ten full minutes apologising. I smiled non-stop all throughout.

Pita ji giggled. That's exactly the kind of thing he would find funny. Once again, what exactly does Ananya see in him?

'See aunty, I told you she is fine,' said Pita ji triumphantly as if he was responsible for the fact that I was alive and breathing.

'Beta,' said mum in a filmy tone turning towards Purva, 'Thank you, beta.'

'*Ek pal mein beta bola agale pal mein hi paraya karr diya,*' said Pita ji smugly. Anu looked proudly at Pita ji.

What the hell was wrong with him! I realised the one advantage of being unconscious is that you get to not listen to Pita ji's nonsense. I thought dreamily of the hours of unconscious sleep where Pita ji and his absolutely lame and random jokes did not exist.

Purva smiled and put a hand on mum's shoulder, 'That's all right aunty. I am glad I could help,' he said. It was then, a little later that my eyes fell on another face in the room.

Rajeev!

The next thought hit me like a tornado. Mom and Rajeev sir in the same room!

'It's OK Kas,' said Rajeev sir coming closer to me and smiling at my mum. Mum looked at Rajeev sir and smiled shyly. Smiled! I mean smiled! I mean like really really smiled! I mean the corners of the lips twitching and teeth showing smile!

Rajeev sir put a hand on mum's shoulder. Mum then put her hand on Rajeev sir's hand. I stared at the bonding in disbelief. Surely a lot has happened since my accident. Last I knew mum would not have anything to do with the 'Punjabi boy' and would much rather see me dead than allow me to marry him.

'Beta, don't worry about Rajeev and me. I like him. I am fine with whatever you guys decide,' said my mother with a ridiculous, almost pious, look on her face.

'Mom! You are the best,' said Rajeev sir winking at mum.

Mom? MOM? Rajeev sir was calling my mother, 'mom'? And on top of that winking at her?

Winking!

And I cannot even get started about the way mum blushed once Rajeev sir winked. Oh my dear lord!

As I stood there befuddled with the turn of events, it hit me like a bolt of lightning. I knew now why mum behaved differently. Seeing me hit and plummeted like a pillow might have mellowed her. So much so that she is even ready to marry me off to a 'pompous Punjabi' after which she will never even be able to lift her eyes in the presence of the rest of the family. That has to be the reason, I thought ruefully.

Rajeev sir came close to me and put his hand on my hand, 'It is all over, sweetheart. You are safe,' he said his brown eyes smiling.

'So why exactly did those people attack Kasturi?' asked Ananya. I looked at her. She seemed to be healing well after the accident and stood right next to Pita ji clutching his hand. We are a rather lucky bunch, are we not? One gets hit by an auto, one gets attacked by the mafia, another jumps into a fight with the mafia and gets hurt, and another has to agree to the match between her rather profligate Brahmin daughter and a Punjabi boy. Oh well, the unfairness of life.

'Because, the men were actually into many illegal things and had been fooling the police for a long time. With so much of focus on the auto guy due to the accident case and your evidence, there was a huge chance of the entire gang being busted. That freaked them out! It seems they had full plans to wipe you off the face of the earth that night. Only they did not know that our Kassie is so damn smart and our Doc here is such a good athlete,' said Pita ji as he playfully poked Purva in the ribs.

Purva cringed as everyone started speaking at the same time about the gangsters and my the attack on me.

24 September 2009

I was amazed by the fact of life coming to a full circle. A few weeks earlier I was cajoling Ananya into walking and now there she was, helping me walk. The same hospital, the same ward and the same doctor.

Another thing that remained constant is Pita ji who continued to be the pain that he has been ever since he came into my life. He has come up with a lot of really dumb and egregious jokes. Here is a sample:

Q: What did the dog say to the tree?

Answer: Hey, bark

I mean like come on. These should be banned.

25 September 2009

9.00 a.m.

Pita ji called up to tell me another one. It goes like this:

Question: What did Batman say to Robin before they got into the car?

Answer: Robin, get in the car.

Again, why exactly did god create Pita ji?

2.00 p.m.

A respectable national daily today brought out an article titled 'Kasturi's Chutzpah'. It talked about my attack and highlighted my bravery. It details how I dealt with the rather difficult situation with complete sangfroid. It described me as 'a spunky young woman'. Only, they missed out the 's' in 'spunky'.

26 September 2009

'Hi,' said Rajeev.

Rajeev popped from behind a lady who had just materialised at our door and smiled, his brown eyes crinkling at their corners making me feel all warm inside.

'Hi,' I said. I was sitting up in my bed flipping through the pages of a Bollywood magazine.

Seeing the unexpected guests mum stood up too.

'Kasturi, ma. Ma, Kasturi,' said Rajeev as he introduced me to the lady standing in front of him.

The first thing I did was to look down at what I was wearing – the hospital gown in dull blue which suddenly seemed positively revolting. The next moment my hands went to my hair, all oily from having not been washed in the longest time ever and then to my face that had only been washed thrice since the accident. I gave up after that. There could be no salvation unless the earth splits up and swallows me.

'Hello aunty,' I stammered.

Rajeev's mom came forward. She was wearing a very elegant, pink sari with a silver border, had done her hair in a plait that reached to her waist and wore light make up. She was by far the most elegant lady I had ever seen. I saw my mum stare fixedly at the sari. I could easily read the look in my mother's face! Mrs Mehrotra had passed the sari test with flying colours!

I then observed Rajeev's mother closely – her warm smile with which she introduced herself to everyone, the intelligent forehead and the perfect white teeth. I felt ugly.

My eyes travelled to hers and stopped short – they were the exact colour as those of her son. The same beautiful light brown that was reminiscent of the deliciousness of chocolate. It took me a second to get over how absolutely identical their eyes were!

'I am sorry I did not know you were coming,' I said apologetically as I saw her looking intently at me – to the girl her only son was in love with.

'That's OK, I told Rajeev not to tell you, I did not want you getting worried,' she said kindly.

'It's very nice of you to come,' said my mother suddenly realising that there was immense possibility of the lady in front of her ending up as her *samdhan*.

'How could I not come?' said Rajeev's mom, 'after all she is *my* daughter as well. I cannot tell you Mrs Shukla, how my heart sank when Rajeev told me about the attack. My poor little girl,' said Rajeev's mom looking at me with sad eyes.

How could mom be left behind? So she went on to claim that Rajeev was the son she never had to which Rajeev's mom agreed and added that I was the daughter *she* never had. Of course by then mom had forgotten all about how she had slammed the door in Rajeev's face that fateful day. He was now a son. A very rich son. With a very elegant mother my mum could proudly show off at family gatherings. It all fits, does not it?

The two mothers started chatting like old friends and very soon I could catch snippets of their conversation which seemed to centre mainly on the shops from where Rajeev's mom bought her saris. Why was I was not surprised?

'Mrs Shukla, I have come here for a purpose,' said Rajeev's mom addressing my mum but facing me. I looked at Rajeev who was sitting on my bed next to my feet. He gave me a smug smile. He knew what was coming. I looked on with interest.

'Yes?' said mum.

'I know my son loves your daughter and what I see and from what I have heard about Kasturi in the last couple of months, I have no doubt in Rajeev's choice. With all humbleness I would like to ask for the hand of your beautiful daughter for my son Rajeev.'

Okay. I think I heard it wrong. I mean like WHAT? Are the mothers discussing my wedding? OH MY GOD! My heart galloped like a very happy horse.

I heard Ananya gasp. Rajeev looked smug and winked at me. I of course, obliged by blushing immediately! So this is where it has finally happened, I thought to myself? In a hospital! Of all the places in the world, in a hospital? While I try to recover from injuries inflicted upon me by respectable members of the underworld? My mum, befittingly, looked too stunned to speak.

'My husband would have come and spoken but he is away on business and will return in December for a week and go back again,' said Rajeev's mom apologetically. She looked so pretty even when she looked apologetic.

'I am happy with the decision the kids have made,' my mum said piously. I knew she was imagining a camera focus on her, the understanding parent of the girl the rich woman's son was madly in love with. The tantrums she had thrown when I had first told her about Rajeev just a few days back seemed to have all evaporated as she lovingly caressed Rajeev's head who comically enough bent low to let mum's hand reach his head.

'Engagement in December then, when Rajeev's dad is in India?' asked Rajeev's mum casually.

'December?' said mum shocked. She gulped twice after that.

'December!' I exclaimed happily!

'Yes, why, you want it earlier?' asked Rajeev's mom asked my mom.

'No no, how will I do the preparations?'

'That's OK. We will do all the preparations…you please don't worry about anything…you just have to come to the venue on the day of the engagement,' the mums yapped on. I could not take my eyes off the handsome man sitting on my bed.

Purva, Ananya and Pita ji congratulated me though only after I caught Ananya exchange a look with Pita ji that I could not quite understand. Within minutes my hospital room turned into the drawing room of the girl's house where she has just been presented to the rich groom's family, been made to walk, talk, sing and bring in chai after which the boy's parents have happily agreed that their son should marry this happily singing, walking and chai bringing girl.

Dad was hurriedly called. He came in all excited and happy bringing sweets for everyone. The nurses and the doctors congratulated Rajeev and me. Everyone was talking with everyone. Dad was frantically making calls to his side of the family.

Like one of the nurses said, our room had to be the happiest room in the entire hospital at that moment.

Just before Rajeev's mom left she turned around and kissed my forehead.

'Welcome to the family, beta,' she whispered.

'Thank you aunty,' I said trying to not imagine how my hair must be smelling.

'When will you start calling me mummy?' she said smiling.

'Right away, mummy,' I said.

In that split second tears filled her beautiful eyes.

'I never thought I would see this day!' she said and straightened up to unclasp the beautiful necklace she was wearing.

'This once belonged to my mother-in-law. I want you to keep it now. You have no idea how happy I am,' she said as she put the necklace around my neck while I was too stunned to speak.

She kissed me once again and left the room.

Mom spent two hours inspecting the necklace and almost died with happiness when we all collectively decided that the white shiny things on it were indeed diamonds.

27 September 2009

The engagement date has been fixed for 29 December, 2009. I am freaking out! I am getting engaged! To Rajeev sir. I will be Mrs Rajeev Mehrotra? Oh My God!!!! Is this really happening?

28 September 2009

I was in the hospital room sitting and leafing through a magazine that had some rather disturbing looking parrot green lehengas that the magazine, rather optimistically, claimed were designed to make the bride look stunning. Pita ji walked in. As usual he had not knocked before entering but I was so tired of telling him off for it that I just kept silent.

Pita ji came and sat at the foot of my bed. He seemed to be in the mood for a talk. He spoke of the finance club at ISB, his current work in trading, the questionable state of the share market and a lot of other things I was not even vaguely interested in.

The willy-nilly talks continued for about half an hour while I pretended to listen and nod. Pita ji paused, paced around the room for a few minutes, gave me a constipated look (which in Pita ji's case meant that he did not quite know how to put into words what he wanted to say) for a few minutes and then walked up to my bed and sat next to me.

He kept quiet for a few minutes while I waited patiently.

'Are you happy Kasturi?' he asked in a quiet voice. So that is why he was blabbering like an idiot! This is what he wanted to ask me. That very instant my so far thoroughly bored heart warmed to the fuzzy, warm, puckish and huggable idiot that Pita ji had time and again turned out to be.

'Yes,' I said honestly. On my lap lay my cell which contained at least fifteen messages Rajeev sir had sent to me in the last two hours.

He smiled.

I smiled.

'Tell me one more thing. Should a good friend be honest?'

'What kind of a question is that?' I asked, perplexed.

'Simple one,' he said. I 'argghhed'-ed mentally.

'Of course, friends should *always* be honest,' I said.

'Ok thanks,' said Pita ji, 'then I have to tell you that you have a crooked nose and when your engagement pictures are being clicked you should make sure it does not get caught in the wrong camera angle.'

I rolled my eyes and set forth to give him a piece of my very indignant mind.

30 September 2009

I am back home! I have still not joined work but I am feeling much better and will get back to it soon.

22

The Weird Request

2 November 2009

Now that I am back home and almost back in good shape, mom has left me in Ananya's care. Since it came about that my attack was linked to Ananya's accident, Ananya had been extremely guilt ridden and has been doing all that she can to make things comfortable for me. Ananya's mom has sent two maids, one car and a driver to be at our beck and all 24X7. We live the life of luxury.

I spent the evening with Ananya and Pita ji playing carom. Once I had had enough of carom and loosing, I was about to call it a day when Pita ji spoke up.

'Kas,' he said, 'you know, if I ask you for something weird will you agree?'

'No,' I said closing the lid on the bottle of talcum powder we had been using to smoothen the surface of the carom board.

'If I say please and Anu also says please then?' he pestered like a two-year-old.

'I will say yes then but it depends on what you want,' I added as a disclaimer.

Ananya and Pita ji exchanged a look I could not quite comprehend.

'Okay, so this is the deal. You know how different married life becomes? We want you to...you know...have some fun before you marry...go shop...have pedicures...you know generally have fun.'

'Okay, that's very sweet of you but Pita ji, tell me what makes you think I won't have pedicures, or fun after I get married?' I asked smiling at how uncomfortable Pita ji looked.

'No...no of course you will have fun...but like Ananya and I want to go to a discotheque with you,' he said now very very uncomfortable.

'What?' I asked surprised. I will never understand Pita ji. I should really stop trying.

'Yes, three times. That's all that I want. So that you can have fun. Also you cannot tell *anyone* about this,' he said as if repeating stuff he had mugged up for an examination.

'Errr...I...just came out of the hospital Pita ji. I am not too sure...,' I said not sure how I could refuse such a weird request.

'Please don't say no, please?' said Ananya who had been quiet all this while.

'Okay,' I said shrugging. Ananya had also become weird. Maybe they have planned a big surprise for me. This was the only logical explanation.

7 November 2009

As per Pita ji's very weird request of secretly taking me to a disc three times before I got engaged, we went out tonight to a disc very suspiciously called Ecstasy.

Yes, so because of dear, considerate friends I went to the disc almost as soon as I could walk again. The two hours we spent there were horribly boring as I had neither the inclination nor a partner to dance with. What made it all the worse was the manner in which Anu and Pita ji behaved all through the evening. They looked very restless and distracted the whole while.

10 November 2009

'How is Teena aunty?' I asked Rajeev murmuring the proverbial sweet nothings into my mobile while on our daily late night call after work. I recalled Rajeev's mother's elegant sari and beautiful face and cringed as my mind wandered to how pathetically ugly I had been looking that day. Mom-in-law and daughter-in-law, what a contrast we will make, I thought ruefully.

'Which Teena aunty,' said Rajeev suddenly sounding stern breaking my line of thought.

'What do you mean by which Teena aunty?' I said surprised at both the question and the tone in which it had been asked. I had often seen 'Teena' engraved in small letters on the underside of his wrist. He had told me Teena was his mum, I could bet my life on it. I remember mentioning that in my diary as well. Plus, I never forget such details.

'I don't know any Teena,' he said a little too angrily.

'You told me your mum is called Teena!' I said baffled.

'No, I did not. Why would I? Her name is Payal,' he said sounding irritated. This did not make sense. Was he lying or had I forgotten something...well...I had to take *his* word for his mother's name.

'Then whose name do you have engraved on your hand?' I asked.

'Not my mum's,' he said trying to laugh it off.

'You still have not answered my question, Rajeev,' I said sternly.

'Sweetheart, it was a joke...nothing more...I did it for fun. See, some guy from college challenged me into doing it...that's all...,' he said.

'Really?' I said still a little incredulous. This was absolutely and rather unwelcome new information.

'Yeah! I was in engineering college...it was a Saturday night...I was a little tipsy...we had been drinking in the college pub when we saw this stranger and my friend challenged me into going up to her, asking her name and the getting that name engraved...I know it's stupid but that's all that there is to the tattoo....,' said Rajeev sir.

'Are you sure that is all,' I asked, still not really believing him. If this was all that was there to the tattoo then why did he lie to me in the first place?

'Yes, so now you do not even trust me?' he said sounding hurt.

'No, no,' I said hurriedly. I was in no mood for a fight but I could not shake off the feeling that there was more to the story than he had just told me. However, Rajeev sir changed the topic to my engagement dress and that made me forget all else. After all what could be more important than that? No, really.

Anyways, the good thing was that my would-be mother-in-law's real name has been revealed to me. The bad thing was that I could not quite shake off something. What, I do not know. Why, I do not know.

12 November 2009

I went to the hospital again to see Purva. For once no one was dying and I just needed a general check-up and an injection. Purva greeted me warmly and after asking a couple of questions about my health left me alone in his cabin to go get my specialist doctor. That was when I first noticed them. The two nurses who had been in the room all this while observing me and Purva.

The nurses were Tamilians and as Purva left they started chatting in their native language quite oblivious, obviously, of the fact that I too am very well versed with the language. In fact, I think I speak better Tamil than most Tamilians. OK, exaggeration. I can hardly speak the language but I have no difficulty in understanding it. Thanks to aai, my Tamilian nanny who took care of me when I was born and continued to cosset and pamper me till I turned eight and decided that slapping aai across her face really hard was a particularly entertaining pastime. And I had a lot of free time.

Aai had showered me with abuses in Tamil as she, flushed with anger left the house for good that day. I still chuckle at the memory.

'Where has he gone? She just needs one simple injection, not her specialist?' asked the short dark nurse in a thick Tamil accent.

'To get Dr Ajay,' said the taller one.

'Why?'

'Where do you live?' asked the taller nurse sounding very exasperated at the limited information the shorter one had about me and Purva, 'This is the same girl, the one whose life the doctor saved. He jumped right in front of the men who were attacking this girl. Risked his own life,' she said as I once again silently thanked Purva for all that he had done for me.

'And you know what?' asked the taller nurse continuing her discourse, 'He has not given her a single injection during her entire treatment. He always gets someone else to give her the injection,' she finished with a very superior, I-know-it-all-and-will-only-tell-things-when-asked look.

I was amazed because now that I thought it over, this bit of observation was absolutely correct.

'Why does he do that?' asked the shorter one.

'You know his mum came to the hospital some time back?' the taller expert on Dr Purva asked the shorter one who nodded so hard that I feared her head would come off her neck.

'He did not give his mother injections either,' said the enlightened one.

'Meaning....,' the shorter one still looked perplexed.

'Ohhoo...you are such a big duffer! Observe Purva when Dr Ajay gives the girl the injection, Purva will turn away his eyes. He always does. He can't see her in pain,' she finished with a meaningful smile.

What? I thought to myself. It sounded so cheesy and...err...umm...and...uummm...

The nurses stopped talking as in walked the doctors. Indeed it was Dr Ajay who was happily chatting with Purva. And sure as hell, Dr Ajay was the one who gave me the injection a couple of minutes later when Purva suddenly became very interested in my case file and did not seem to have the few seconds needed for the injection.

Not to be outdone, I fought against all forces of nature and kept my eyes open wide as the needle went inside my skin to see Purva. And sure enough, Purva turned away his head as the needle went inside my arm. I think I saw him cringe then and noticed how many times he asked me if it had hurt.

Apart from that, Purva's behaviour was impeccable. He seemed concerned but not too concerned... just the way a good friend should be. He insisted on walking me to the door and seeing me inside Ananya's car.

13 November 2009

9.00 p.m.

My phone rang.

'Kassie?' said Pita ji sounding all excited. Not happy excited just weird excited.

'Yeah?' I said.

'What are you doing?'

'Nothing much,' I said staring at my pyjamas and the ice cream tub that I had been digging into. My fifth for the week. The rate at which I was eating big, huge tubs of ice cream would have ensured that I bear a distinct resemblance to a football on the engagement day. The thought disturbed me to the core and I set aside the ice cream tub. 'Where is Rajeev?' Pita Ji asked urgently.

'Office. He is staying late to work,' I said. I had spoken to Rajeev some two hours back. He had told me that he would be working late and we might not be able to have our late night call. Aaah, well, the sacrifices I make for my fiancé-to-be's career. I have to be the most devoted girlfriend on planet earth.

'Great, then why don't you come with me? Ananya is getting her mom's car and driver and we are going on your second disc trip.'

'What!' I said, in no mood to get out of my comfortable bed and pyjamas.

'Yes!'

'No! I am not well,' I fibbed.

'I do not care,' the line went dead.

Great, I thought to myself as I pulled myself unwillingly out of the bed.

9.30 p.m.

Ananya met me in the hallway. She looked oddly nervous and listless. I think they are a good match. Mr Weird and Ms Weird and when they marry they shall be Mr and Mrs Weird.

10.15 p.m.

So we have reached the now familiar Ecstasy disc again. Since I was not interested in coming out in the first place, I am wearing plain jeans and a simple pink top.

Ananya continues to act weird.

I even heard her murmuring to herself which is something she does only when she is tense. I think I heard her mutter something about not knowing what to wish for. I think she is hiding something from me yet again. This never augers well. I am feeling a little uneasy now.

10.30 p.m.

I am in the disc and am surrounded with people gyrating their sweaty bodies to loud music. Sweat.

Music that's too loud.

People who are too drunk.

I don't feel safe. The attack has changed me forever. This place would not have affected me one month back but today I feel unsafe and want to get away as soon as I can.

10.32 p.m.

My heart stopped beating for a second. I thought I saw someone I knew in the sea of bodies gyrating to the music. The next second no one was there. I breathed easy.

10.45 p.m.

I am a great fan of Pepsi. I think in my life so far I must have consumed equal amounts of water and Pepsi. I firmly believe that the global sales figures for Pepsi will show a considerable dip if I stop drinking it. I am not kidding; I even made a graph once to prove my point to Varun in office.

The problem with drinking excessive water/Pepsi is the very inconvenient increase in the frequency of required loo breaks.

I was, thus, walking away from the crowd and towards the ladies room when I heard a girl squeal. I could not see anyone around and had decided to disregard the noise when it came again. This time my heart skipped a beat. What if some girl needed help? I don't know why the attack incident kept coming back to me again and again tonight. It was making me feel extremely uneasy and I just wanted the night to end.

10.46 p.m.

Following the sound, I walked around the ladies room to a quiet dark corner behind it. I relaxed as I heard the girl giggle now.

10.47 p.m.

My fear of finding a girl being attacked by random men subsided as the girl continued to giggle and squeal with delight. I could now make out the frames of two people entwined into each other in the badly lit corner.

Not up to any good, I thought grimly to myself like the grandmother who disapproves of the grand daughter's mini skirt. In that moment, I missed Rajeev like crazy. I had this incredible urge of waking off from the disc to Rajeev's office just to sit next to him and hold his hand. Sometimes I just miss him too much even when he is a feet away. I was amazed at the amount of love I feel for Rajeev sir.

10.48 p.m.

I was about to walk away when I heard another voice. That voice alone would have made me stop dead. Let alone what it said. In one of the most incredible co-incidences of my life, the voice belonged to the very person I had been thinking about seconds ago.

I turned around and squinted to see the frame that belonged to the other voice. Even though it was dark, there was no mistaking Rajeev's frame and voice as it murmured Teena's name.

10.49

I stayed there for a second not able to breathe. I felt claustrophobic.

10:49:30

I cleared my throat.

'Rajeev,' I called out hoping for no answer.

The four hands and legs separated instantly dashing my last ray of hope in the same instant.

Rajeev walked out of the darkness along with a tall, skinny, drunk looking girl. Rajeev's face turned pale. For once his eyes looked mean and calculating. Where was the warmth I always saw in them?

'Kasturi! What are you doing here?' he said his face and lips still white.

'I think I can ask that question to the man I am about to get engaged to soon,' I said oddly calm.

'Was this really happening? Maybe this was another of those weird dreams I have been having ever since the attack.' I thought to myself.

'I...ummm...nothing, I was talking to my friend here,' stammered the man in whom till now I had not been able to find a single fault. My world seemed to have crashed.

'Your friend called Teena?' I asked again with tremendous calm.

'Hi, Kassie,' chirped drunk Teena, 'I luurvvve Raju!'

I turned away disgusted and started walking away from the duo as if in a trance. Pita ji, Varun and Ananya were standing outside the clearing. I vaguely wondered how Varun had managed to come here. I walked towards them not really aware of where I was going. My brain seemed to have stopped working. What had just happened? Why had it happened? I think Rajeev came after me, tried to hold me back but I pushed him away.

Pita ji came between me and Rajeev.

'Please leave her alone now, Rajeev. Let her be,' said Pita ji in a calm quiet voice, the unexpected authority of which took Rajeev by surprise. Ananya came to stand by me and so did Varun. With Pita ji in front of me and Varun and Anu on both sides, my friends had surrounded me in my darkest hour.

I heard the tapping of high heels as Teena came tottering after Rajeev. She put her arms around Rajeev and planted a sloppy, wet kiss on his cheeks. Rajeev sir pushed her aside and looked at me with guilt ridden eyes. I turned away in disgust.

'I will kill both of them, Anu,' I said looking at Ananya with helpless angry tears in my eyes.

'Let's go, Kas,' said Varun quietly.

'Kasturi!' shouted Rajeev in a painful voice 'please wait!'

I turned back to face my cheating fiancé-to-be.

'I will if you can tell me why you did this,' I said taking angry steps towards him and waving a hand towards the drunk girl, 'and why you lied about this,' I said pointing to his wrist that read the name of the same drunk girl, 'and why I was supposed to believe that you are in office at the present moment. What am I now supposed to think of the night when Anu met with the accident and you were with 'friends' the whole while ignoring my frantic calls, and what about the fact that it was not you but Purva who helped me from those men. Why was it Purva and not you sitting next to me when I first opened my eyes after the attack,' I screamed madly, a purgative exercise.

Varun and Ananya came up to me and put their arms around me in a failed attempt to quieten me.

'Why Rajeev, why?' I screamed at the top of my voice, tears streaming down my face. My perfect world around the perfect Rajeev had crashed in one quick loo break in a matter of a few seconds.

'Kasturi, I love you!' Rajeev pleaded sounding so fake that I felt anger surge inside me in a fresh wave I could do nothing to stop.

Jerking off Ananya and Varun's restraining hands, I went up to Rajeev and with great purpose did something that I had never before in my life even thought of.

Mustering up all my strength, hatred and anger, like a woman possessed, I raised my hand and slapped Rajeev hard across his face ten times without stopping.

23

The Ramifications of a Weird Request

14 November 2009

No. of calls from Rajeev: 58; No. of calls answered: 0
No. of calls from dad: 5; No. of calls answered: 0
No. of texts from Rajeev: 23; No. of texts replied to: 0
No. of knocks on my door: 45; No. of knocks answered: 0
No. of hours cried: 24

15 November 2009

I was drafting my resignation letter when in slipped a letter from under the door.

Written in Ananya's hand, it read as follows:

'Dearest Kasturi,

While there is a lot Varun, Amu and I want to say right now, we are limited by words that do not do justice to how we feel.

I have heard your sobs for one whole day and while I knew

this was inevitable it is more difficult to see you like this than any of us had imagined. It breaks my heart into a million pieces each time I stand next to your door hoping you would open it this one time.

What makes us feel very guilty is that it was us who took you to the club. Not just that, the very purpose in taking you there, unfortunately, was to enable you to witness what you saw. Your state, therefore, is our fault. And we cannot even describe how we feel about it. But please read what I now write with patience.

Rajeev's cousin sister, Radha, is seeing Amu's brother. I have personally met Radha a couple of times and during one such dinner, Radha told us about Rajeev, her handsome brother who was creating a lot of problems for the family due to his wayward ways. It did not take me much time to realise that this Rajeev was the same Rajeev Mehrotra from office. I did not then know that you were seeing Rajeev sir, and it was just out of curiosity that I prodded Radha further. It was then that I found out that Rajeev was seeing a girl called Teena, whom he had been dating for the last five years and wished to marry. His mother was dead opposed to the match as she considered Teena to be a girl with no worthy qualities. She made it clear that Rajeev could marry Teena only if he were fine with severing all ties with the family, something that Rajeev could never even think of doing. In all fairness, Rajeev loves his mother to death and could not bear to go against her wish that seemed set in cement.

Rajeev who works in our office probably just to get some extra pocket money or to keep himself busy has a huge family business which would have been out of bounds as well had he gone ahead with Teena who is, by the way, known to be addicted to both alcohol and drugs. Anyways, whatever the factors at play, Rajeev confided to Radha that he would find a girl his mother would approve of and get married. Teena would remain Rajeev's love and a part of his life even after the marriage. Teena was fine with this arrangement and all that was left was to find a suitable girl. Radha went on to tell me that from what her brother had confided in her, he had managed to find someone in his office that he kind of liked and was sure his mom would love.

Ironically when I had called you and Varun to Select City Mall to tell you guys about Amay, I was intending to share this bit of office gossip with you. Only I never really got the chance.

I met with the accident before I got to meet you guys and when I regained consciousness, I found that you were seeing Rajeev sir. You were the girl Radha had been telling me about. You, Kasturi, you.

While it shocked me to the core, I did not know how to tell you. And I cannot apologise enough for that. In retrospect that was a mistake and would have saved you a lot of heartache. I don't think you can or should forgive me for this.

But in my defence, I saw how much you loved Rajeev sir and more importantly how Rajeev seemed to be the perfect boyfriend. I observed how Rajeev reciprocated your feelings which confused me quite a bit. Maybe Radha had wrong information. There were immense possibilities and each time my brain told me to go tell you, my heart found some glimmer of hope.

Confused, I confided in Amu and Varun. In the meanwhile your mum refused to allow you to marry Rajeev. That gave us some time to think and find out stuff through Radha as we knew you would find a way around aunty soon enough.

Before we could figure anything out for you, your attack happened and our priorities completely changed in a matter of seconds. I have never been able to tell you how I felt after your attack which in the first place happened solely because of me. I was guilt ridden and devastated. I spent hours crying in the temple praying for your recovery. All the while feeling all the more scared about telling you the truth about Rajeev sir. I felt I was just continuously bringing you bad luck. However, after your attack and while you were in the hospital, though Rajeev was not there as often as he should have been, for the time that he was there, he seemed completely devoted to you and I felt quite confused.

As abruptly as most things had happened so far, your mum agreed to the wedding and before our stunned eyes Rajeev's mom who was only too happy to have you for a daughter-in-law and in a hurry lest, I now realise, the story got out, came and fixed the engagement date.

With the engagement date so near, we did not know what to do or say. We could have just told you but we also knew that so strong was your faith in Rajeev that you would never believe what we had to say. We also knew through Radha that Rajeev frequented Ecstasy with Teena very often and that is why we took you there. We had decided that we will

*take you there thrice, if we happened to chance upon them
you would see it for yourself and know beyond a shadow
of doubt what Rajeev was up to. However, if that had not
happened, we had planned to come up to you to tell you
all we knew.*

*Inspite of all that has happened and what we now know to
be true, I actually believe though Amu and Varun disagree,
that in his own way Rajeev did fall in love with you. But I
also know that you deserve better. You deserve much better.
A nice kind man who would love you and only you.*

*I am not going to preach you about how finding out stuff
about Rajeev was the best thing that could have happened to
you. No, you do not deserve that crap. Cry as much as you
want to, be as angry as you feel like, throw things around,
scream at us, shout at us, hit us, just get Rajeev and all that
he stood for out of your system. Think about it and please
please please come out of your room. Please.*

*I am sorry Kas, I wish with all my heart that things had
turned out differently for you and Rajeev. I wish with all
my heart that friendship with me had not brought you so
many problems, so much pain, such great heartbreak. I am
sorry. I am very sorry.*

*But having said that I have to tell you that you are the
nicest, kindest, loveliest person I have ever known. I would
happily take all your heartbreak if it was possible. I love you,
Kasturi. You are the best friend I have ever had and cannot
bear the thought of you going away from my life.*

*You might choose to not speak to any of us. I will try and
understand that, Kasturi. But like I said, you are my best
friend and will always remain one.*

*I will always stand by you. Always. No matter what comes
our way.*
With all the love in our hearts,
Anu
Amay
Varun

I read the note five times all the while standing by the door. The
last few lines tugged at my heart. The letter explained so many
things, big and small. The way Rajeev showered me with such
attention in the very beginning that transformed my harmless crush
into sincere love, the all too frequent trips to 'Chandigarh,' the
late night work hours, the ignoring of my phone calls, the making
sure that his mobile was always with him and never withen my
reach, the hurry to get married that I stupidly mistook for love,
the pride with which he showed me off to his mother that I again
mistook for love, the tears in his mother's eyes when she told me
that she had never thought this day would come...

I had no doubt that each word in Anu's letter was true. I
imagined the guilt poor Anu had been living in and inexplicably,
I also understood how difficult it must have been for her to come
up to me and tell me about Rajeev sir. I know how madly in
love I was with Rajeev. I felt an immense sense of gratitude not
only for Anu but also towards Varun and more importantly Pita ji
who in a way saved my life. Imagine what would have happened
had I actually married Rajeev? I felt shivers down my spine as I
studied the scenario.

I was wiping away tears when I heard a soft, timid knock
on the door.

I hesitated for a second and then opened the door. Ananya
was standing there with Pita ji and Varun a little behind her.

Seeing tears streaming down my face and the letter in my hand a little sob escaped Ananya.

'I am sorry Kas,' she said, her eyes welling up with tears as she walked towards me.

Pita ji, looking grave himself, took a step forward and hugged me tight without saying a single word. Varun had tears streaming down his face as he came forward and hugged the two of us. Seconds later Ananya wiggled in as well. I smiled through my tears and the four of us hugged tight. In that moment for the first time since the time I set my eyes on Teena, who by the way, I hope rots in hell along with Rajeev, I felt that I would be able to live through this…

17 November 2009

The door bell rang. I waited for Ananya to open the door – she was on leave. When the bell rang again after a few minutes, I reluctantly got out of my bed and opened the door to see Purva standing there.

'Hey!' I said surprised as I had not expected him at all.

'Hi, good time to come in?' he asked looking closely at me.

'Yeah, sure…,' I said as I opened the door further to let him in.

'Are you OK?' he asked as we sat down on the sofas in the drawing room.

'Yes,' I smiled weakly. I have been worse. With support from Anu, Pita ji and Varun I am trying to rebuild my life that currently lies shattered somwehere in the depths of nowhere. I still am not taking any calls from Rajeev and had sent him his mom's necklace through Ananya yesterday. I did receive a huge 100 GB mail from him. I read each and every word and finding nothing in it that seemed genuine or heartfelt, deleted it with disgust.

'Hmm...I just thought I will catch up with you,' he said. I had a feeling that he had some background on what had happened through Ananya.

'How did you know I was not at office?' I asked.

'Because I know you have resigned,' he said calmly.

I looked down. I knew what was coming.

'Purva...,' I said not sure whether I would be able to tell him the whole story without breaking down.

'Yes?' he said as he inched closer, his eyes filled with concern.

A big huge tear started its familiar journey down my cheeks.

'Kasturi! What happened?' said Purva as my quiet tears grew into full blown tears and sobbing. And with that the whole story came out. I spent over an hour telling Purva about all that had happened. The afternoon spilled into evening and we kept on talking, or rather I kept on speaking, speaking my heart out, purging myself and my soul of Rajeev. Purva listened patiently to each word I said. It was the first time I was speaking about this to someone and I felt oddly light after having done so.

'Do you still love him Kasturi?' he asked me.

'No,' I said after giving it some thought.

'Do you realise that he was probably never really yours?' he asked.

'Yes and that hurts,' I said.

'Do you think you will get over him?' he asked after a pause.

'No,' I said, again after giving it some thought.

Purva smiled and for the first time ever, put an arm around me, 'You will be fine, Kasturi,' he said smiling.

'I honestly do not think so, Purva,' I said shaking my head.

He paused for sometime.

'Kasturi?' he said.

I looked up. He looked intently at me for a few seconds. I could sense his eyes follow a big fat tear down my face. He seemed to decide something.

'No nothing,' he said.

After that we sat in a comfortable silence for a long time. Purva switched on the tv and we watched couple of episodes of *FRIENDS*. This absolute all time favourite series somehow failed to divert my mind which kept thinking on and on about what Rajeev had done and why he had done so.

I sat on the couch not seeing what was happening on tv when I realised that Purva was heading towards the kitchen.

'Oh I am sorry!' I said slapping my forehead, 'What would you like to have, tea or coke?'

'No, I don't want you to get me anything; I am going to cook us some lunch.'

'No!' I exclaimed.

'Why?'

'I am not hungry,' I said sulking.

'Oh,' he said grimacing, 'I thought that you were going to play host and get up and cook something for me!' he said laughing now.

I rolled my eyes at him smiling weakly.

'Aaah...fine, then can I make something for myself?' he asked.

'Yeah, of course, the kitchen is all yours,' I said readily.

Purva spent the next few minutes cutting up onions, sautéing them with cumin seeds and then adding them to Maggie.

I sniffed the lovely familiar smell of Maggie and my stomach growled.

Purva took his bowl of Maggie and came into the living room. He placed the bowl of Maggie on the table and put a fork in it.

'That smells lovely! I cannot wait to finish it off,' he said admiring his handiwork.

'Yes sure,' I said.

'You are not going to have any, right,' he said rhetorically.

'No...no,' I said hastily, eyeing the bowl.

'Just in case,' said Purva as he fished out another fork from somewhere and put it in the bowl.

Purva then concentrated on his Maggie and ate it hungrily. I smelled it again, let my drama be, picked up the fork and asked Purva to keep the Maggie bowl in between us.

From the corner of my eye I could see Ananya lean against the door to the drawing room. She was smiling. This was the first time I had seen her smile since the Rajeev thing happened.

I realised with a start that I was smiling too. I stopped short; it seemed strange to be smiling...and I suddenly remembered how Purva had fed me in a similar manner a couple of months ago on that dark night when Anu had met with her accident.

I turned around to look at Ananya.

I smiled again. She came forward not taking her eyes off the bowl of Maggie which suddenly seemed very small.

'Seems yummmm!' she said as she snatched the fork from my hands and slurped happily.

Purva and I exchanged a look like proud parents observing their three month old bundle of joy gurgling and eating his own toes.

I smiled again, it was broader than before. Friends. How much they matter. And how great a difference they can make, no matter how tough the going gets. The world did not seem as grey and I felt a little less lonely.

Maggie does that to you.

24

Happily Ever After?

Present Day

I smiled as I confidently hailed the auto. I could not help but recall how scared I had become of autos after the attack and how one fine day Purva took me all over Delhi in multiple autos to help me overcome my fear.

A lot of things have changed. For starters, I now work with a start up, as their marketing manager. They pay me much less than India Telecom Pvt Ltd did but I do much more than making PPTs, getting photocopies and flirting with my boss. And trust me, this is much better! The cherry on this professional cake is a repulsive, balding, sixty-year-old boss whom I love to hate and spend many happy hours finding faults with.

The auto ride was a long one, but this was now a journey that was very familiar. We live in different parts of the city and AIMMS is almost equidistant for most of us. After we finish work if time permits we meet up in the AIMMS canteen for a catch up that often involves a lot of leg pulling, a gazillion PJs and sometimes dinner.

By we, I mean, Ananya, Pita ji, Varun, Purva and Ajay. Ajay.

Wait a second! You do not know Ajay. Well, actually you do! He is Purva's friend and like him a doctor at AIMMS. Well, between now and the last time I made an entry in the diary, amongst the million things that have happened, Varun's coming out of the closet has pretty much been the highlight. Yes, you heard it right. Varun is seeing Ajay. They are a couple. And no, we had no idea Varun was gay. And, yes, it was as much a surprise to us as it was to his parents. Their dreams of the beta-bahu heaven have been replaced by the potential beta-damaad reality! I think one whole book can be solely dedicated to Ajay and Varun's story.

As I settled in the auto, my mind went back to the absolute, worthy of any tv serial *tamasha* my horrified and hence extremely melodramatic mother did when she found out the truth about Rajeev. It took me a couple of days to muster up enough strength to call up mum to tell her that Rajeev was a cheating, moth-eating, bloody piece of decaying flesh. Anyways, in a matter of seconds, Rajeev went from being a 'very nice, how-does-it-matter-if-he-is-not-a-Brahmin-but-a-Punjabi-boy' to the 'rascal-who-should-be-cut-into-a-million-little-pieces'. She lost no time in calling up Rajeev's mother with whom, by the way, she had become great buddies and calling off the engagement. She then abused the entire family in a loud screechy voice using such colourful abuses that I could not help but giggle even while in the middle of what was undoubtedly the lowest point in my life.

As my auto neared the hospital, I smiled at the memory of how my mother, of all possible things, had called Rajeev's mother a 'colourful and vain peacock'. That was what had made me giggle, I recalled absently.

Mom and dad. My rocks. My pillars of strength. Dad had always been one, the surprise package this time was mum. I recalled how she literally, and much to Anu's initial dismay, shifted base to Delhi for almost a month after my break-up since I refused point blank to go home. She was with me in my sorrow and the two of us have come off much better and closer.

My cell beeped, cutting my line of thought. It was a message from Ananya. She would be a little late in reaching the canteen. Pita ji would come with her.

Ananya and Pita ji. I smiled as I thought about them. I had never in my dreams imagined that at a point in time I would almost owe my life to these two idiots! Along with Purva and Varun, they have been instrumental in my being able to collect myself and start afresh after the disaster Rajeev was or could have been. In the weeks after my break-up, curled up on the sofa and crying nonstop over what could have been, I would often see Anu's eyes brim with tears too. Poor Anu, she went through hell with me and never let go of my hand for even a second. Pita ji who took to calling me a variety of rather disturbing names like 'darling,' 'sweetie' and 'hun' was in his own idiotic, fumbling way a big support. He spent hours with me rationalising why what happened had happened for the best. In the initial days, the two almost stopped going on dates and spent every possible second with me and for weeks after I started feeling much better simply refused to go out without me!

I made my way to Purva's cabin. He was as I had expected wrapping up some work which he needed to submit by the end of his shift. I decided to hang around in his cabin while he scribbled long, dangerous looking words in the huge register.

There was a plastic curtain that divided his cabin from the rest of the room. I heard two nurses walk in. I could make out their silhouettes. One tall and the other short.

'Where is Dr Purva?' said the short one in Tamil. I turned my heard sharply. The voices and the Tamil accent were unexpectedly familiar! These were the two nurses whom I had overheard speaking the other day when I had come for a check-up much before the Rajeev sir fiasco! I was immediately alert as I recalled that Purva and I were their favourite topic of discussion. So what news would they bring for me today, I wondered playfully ready for some fun.

'Rounds,' said the taller, enlightened one with all the answers.

'That pretty girl, I saw her come in again today,' said the shorter one.

'Her name is Kasturi,' informed the taller one. Me, the pretty girl? I smiled to myself, happy with the unexpected compliment. I have always been a big fan of over hearing people's conversations. This flattering compliment reinstated my faith in the noble cause.

'Why does she come here so often? To meet doctor is it?' asked the shorter one.

'The whole gang gets together,' said the taller one irritated by the shorter one's lack of knowledge.

'Ohhh...that ways,' said the shorter one as if this one line made it all crystal clear.

'No!' said the taller one sharply.

'Then?'

'It's not that way,' curtly replied the taller one with a PhD on me and Purva.

'Then?' asked the shorter one, eager for more gossip. Even I inched a little closer to the curtain. Which way was it then?

'Purva is in love with the girl,' said the taller one firmly with a finality in her tone that shook me.

Surprised even though it was coming from some arbit nurse, I turned to look sharply at Purva. With his head bent low he seemed to be scribbling fiercely. Too fiercely. The biggest giveaway were the ears. They were a bright shade of red! Oh my god! He knows Tamil. And wait a second! Does he LOVE me? Like *love* me?

'Really,' said the shorter nurse amazed at the revelation, 'How do *you* know?' she said challenging the taller one's authority.

'Dr Ajay and Dr Purva were discussing that girl Kasturi when I overheard,' the taller nurse divulged her source of information.

'You heard Dr Purva say this himself?' asked the shorter one not believing. And frankly speaking this had me as well. While the nurses could say anything they wanted, was it possible that Purva had actually said this to Ajay?

'Yes…almost, Dr Ajay was pulling his leg about Kasturi and Dr Purva said that he likes her but he was not sure if Kasturi likes him too.'

'Do you think she likes him?'

'She loves him, in her own way, she will find out in some time even if she does not know now,' said the tailer one in a firm and stern voice. I almost felt as if I was being scolded by her for not having figured out that I was in love with Purva.

Purva cleared his throat loudly. Loud enough for the nurses to hear and shut up before they said anything else. He then quickly gathered his papers, put his pen in his pocket, put on his watch and looked at me with a rather uncomfortable smile.

'Let's go?' he asked. He seemed to be in a hurry to get out of the room.

I nodded and we started walking together in silence. We walked across the gardens of AIMMS lit up with the pretty orange pink hues of the sky. Beautiful, green and serene the beauty of the gardens wasted on me as I walked absently, lost in my thoughts and there were many. Purva...the staid, silent and calm doctor my mother had forced me to meet all those months ago...once a potential groom and now pretty much my closest friend...the one man I held in the highest esteem...I recalled the measured interest he had always shown in whatever I did or said...the unquestioned help that he had always provided me with...the way he had risked his life to save mine...would he, no would anyone do that for just a friend? Had I been blind all this while, chasing a man who did not love me while ignoring a man who loved me enough to risk his own life to save mine.

OK. Wait. Purva had not said *anything* yet!

We had walked a little distance when Purva slowed his steps.

'Do you by any chance know Gujarati?' he asked trying to sound very casual.

'No,' I said surprised at the weird question. Why was Purva behaving like Pita ji?

'Hmm...Telugu?' he asked.

'No, but I do know Tamil,' I said smiling as I realised where his seemingly weird questions were heading. He turned around his head sharply so that he faced me. His face looked pained and constipated. I could not help but giggle.

'What?! You know Tamil?' he said horrified as he realised that I had heard and understood all that the nurses had said.

'Yes, and I guess you do too,' I said quite enjoying the situation.

He nodded his head. He did not say anything for some time. My head had too much going on inside it. Purva? Judging by his reaction now, did he really love me?

'Kasturi,' he said turning to face me, 'Please don't bother with what those women were saying.'

'Is it true?' I asked raising my recently threaded and hence hopefully perfectly arched eyebrows.

He looked at me, confused, not knowing what to say. He stayed quiet for a few minutes as if weighing his reply. Finally he decided to speak.

'Kasturi,' he said looking strained and concentrating as if working with a particularly difficult patient, 'it's not now...I...I...have always liked you and with time this feeling has only grown.'

I looked into his eyes. They were sincere and honest. I sensed there was more he wanted to say. I waited for him.

'I tried telling you once or twice but then decided against it. And then Rajeev came in...I know you do not feel the same way for me, Kasturi...and...and...I am fine with it,' he said smiling now. The weight seemed to have lifted from his shoulders.

I kept quiet for some time.

'And you are fine with it?' I asked him.

Purva stared at me for a second and burst out laughing. I turned my face away from him unsure of how I was feeling.

'I am right in thinking that there is no possibility of an 'us,' right...like us getting married or something?' he said sounding unsure. It was part question-part statement. Purva had always been the one I had turned to in despair, it was weird to see him wait for my answer. I took a few seconds before replying.

Does my heart beat crazily for Purva, the way it did for Rajeev? No.

Do my eyes always search for Purva's, the way they did for Rajeev's? No.

Do I think about Purva, the way I always did about Rajeev? No.

I do not love Purva. And I should not marry for anything less.

'No,' I said aloud feeling very uneasy and uncomfortable. There was something wrong with my answer. Also, if he is fine with me not having any feelings for him, then well...so be it.

Purva looked up as I finished my sentence.

'No? No, there is a possibility or no, there cannot be any possibility?' he asked not sure he got what I had said.

And I again started thinking.

Does my heart beat crazily for Purva, the way it did for Rajeev? No, but Purva calms and quietens my heart, mind and soul like Rajeev never could.

Do my eyes always search for Purva's, the way they did for Rajeev's? No, but Purva's are always looking into mine, understanding my fears, apprehensions and aspirations better than Rajeev could ever hope to.

Do I want to spend each waking moment with Purva, the way I did with Rajeev? No, but Purva has, without fail, been with me in each moment of desperation when Rajeev was often conspicuous by his absence.

The answer became clear. I breathed deep and happy. I suddenly felt very relaxed.

'No, I think there *is* a possibility,' I said smiling to myself. I knew this time my answer was right. I was rather surprised at the revelation.

'Really?' he said sounding incredulous.

'Yes,' I said, 'I think there is a possibility,' I repeated slowly.

He had a serious look but it betrayed his happiness. Purva was quiet for a minute. He then took a step back, turned around so that his back was facing me, jumped in the air, clicked his heels mid air, pumped his fists and shouted 'Yes!'!

He then turned around to beguile me with that serene, doctor mask on his face.

'Yes, so you were saying...,' he said calmly in perfect English. I started laughing. He could be such an idiot at times.

'Kasturi,' he said after watching me gurgle with laughter for a few minutes.

I looked up into his eyes that were a boring shade of black. However, I could not but feel a strong sense of security and honesty emanate from them.

'I know you do not love me...,' he said in a low voice that I strained my ears to hear, 'so...so...I will not even ask that question. But...there is something more important than that that I need an honest answer to.'

'Yes?'

'I know you do not love me now, Kasturi, but do you think, one day you will be able to love me?' he asked.

Yes, unfortunately you are right, Dr Purva Dikshit. And well done on the incisive thinking. I do not love you the way you are talking about right now. But I do love you as a friend. I love you and I trust you. I have over the last couple of months seen enough of your friendship to know for a fact that no one will love me more than you will. I have been stupid to ignore it before. Sadly being stupid is not unknown to me. I have been stupid enough to fall for a guy who was hollow and a cheat.

And you ask me if I will be able to love you with all my heart one day?

'Yes,' I said now smiling shyly. I had to be shy. I mean this was a guy proposing, for god's sake. Proposing a proposal that I was accepting! All girls in tv serials wear salwar-suits and smile shyly when the guy proposes.

'Ok. Great,' said Purva not knowing what to say or do. At that moment a thought struck me making me feel uncomfortable.

'Purva,' I said sounding a little unsure.

Purva immediately looked at me, concern written all over his face, 'Yes?' he said.

'I don't want to be anyone's girlfriend. I am done with that,' I said. Purva thought for half a second before answering.

'That's not a problem, Kasturi,' he said as he pulled me into a quiet rather dark corner. The next second he was precariously balancing himself on one knee as I stared open mouthed looking, I am sure, a lot like Pita ji. Oh My God! The mighty, grand Dr Purva Dikshit was going on one knee!

'Kasturi…err…will you ma…err…marry…me and…b…be my…wi…wife?' he said stammering more with each letter and almost tripping over as he finished the sentence. I instinctively went on my knees to support him lest he fell over.

So there we were, in the gardens of AIMMS, next to the famous red wall, both of us on our knees, staring into each other's eyes with my hand on his arm, supporting him.

It was a far cry from what an ideal proposal should be. And the girl medical students passing by giggling uncontrollably at the sight did not really help but Purva spoke with such childlike earnestness and sincerity that it made me smile and for the first time feel something like love for him. He just looked so adorably sweet.

'Yes, so that I can be with you all my life,' I said the next instant more in an attempt to rhyme with what he had said than anything else. His face broke into a smile as did mine.

'I will get the parents speaking…,' he said getting up and dusting the knees of his pants. I nodded. And with some surprise I realised that in the quietest, stupidest, silliest way possible, after all the weird boys I had met, the boyfriend that I had found, I had just decided who I was going to marry. No flurry of emotions as with Rajeev sir, just honest thoughts. It seemed like the right thing. It was not a teenage crush that Rajeev sir had been. Purva is a sensible, honest man. I will love him soon for what he is, I told myself.

We started walking towards where we knew Ananya and Pita ji were waiting for us. Purva's hand touched mine. He instinctively withdrew his hand. But the next instant better sense prevailed and I soon felt his fingers twirling around mine as both of us stared ahead avoiding each other's eyes. Beetroot red in colour (I have no doubt) I did not know where to look and turned my attention to his hands now firmly holding mine in a comfortable grip. The scars caught my attention. The familiarity struck me yet again. Where had I seen them before, much before I met him…where? And then, just like that, it hit me like a bolt lightning. I was dazzled by the answer.

'Purva! When did you see me first?' I asked looking intently at him. Purva's face broke into a smile.

'At Dilli Haat,' he said smiling mischievously.

'No, before that!' I insisted getting agitated. His smile broadened.

'So you figured it out now!' he said laughing now, 'I was wondering if you ever would!'

'Yes! This was the hand that helped me get up from the floor when I had gone to meet Pita ji for the first time and had fallen flat on my face in Big Chill!' I exclaimed loudly holding his hand and staring at the scars, 'the scars on your hand! I remember them now! That's where I saw them!!' I was literally screaming with excitement. I had just solved the biggest mystery of my life!

'You were such a sight then!' Purva said laughing, 'the little oreo shake puddle you had created for yourself!' And for the first time ever I smiled at that cringe worthy memory. So that was where Purva and I actually met first! That fateful day not only did I meet the idiotic but lovable Pita ji but also Purva! Befittingly, Purva had come to my rescue even before he had entered my life. It seemed like a sign from god. I breathed a huge, happy sigh. I could not stop grinning.

So, there I was, hand in hand with a guy I had met first on mum's insistence while I was on a 'date' with another guy, became friends with while seeing *another* guy, came to know of his true feelings for me because of garrulous Tamil speaking nurses... and I felt the happiest I had ever been.

'Will it be happily ever after for us?' my mind questioned as we walked with his hand clutching mine as tightly as it could.

And pat came the reply, loud and clear.

'With Purva, most certainly, YES!'